WE'RE SAFE
WHEN WE'RE
ALONE

WE'RE SAFE WHEN WE'RE ALONE

Nghiem Tran

COFFEE HOUSE PRESS
Minneapolis
2023

Coffee House Press books are available to the trade through our primary distributor, Consortium Book Sales & Distribution, cbsd.com or (800) 283-3572. For personal orders, catalogs, or other information, write to info@coffeehousepress.org.

Coffee House Press is a nonprofit literary publishing house. Support from private foundations, corporate giving programs, government programs, and generous individuals helps make the publication of our books possible. We gratefully acknowledge their support in detail in the back of this book.

LIBRARY OF CONGRESS CATALOGING-IN-PUBLICATION DATA

Names: Tran, Nghiem, 1993– author.
Title: We're safe when we're alone / Nghiem Tran.
Other titles: We are safe when we are alone
Description: Minneapolis : Coffee House Press, 2023.
Identifiers: LCCN 2022055964 (print) | LCCN 2022055965 (ebook) | ISBN 9781566896832 (paperback) | ISBN 9781566896849 (epub)
Subjects: LCGFT: Ghost stories. | Bildungsromans. | Novellas.
Classification: LCC PS3620.R36268 W47 2023 (print) | LCC PS3620.R36268 (ebook) | DDC 813/.6—dc23/eng/20230124
LC record available at https://lccn.loc.gov/2022055964
LC ebook record available at https://lccn.loc.gov/2022055965

PRINTED IN THE UNITED STATES OF AMERICA

30 29 28 27 26 25 24 23   1 2 3 4 5 6 7 8

The NVLA series is an artistic playground where authors challenge and broaden the outer edges of storytelling. Each novella illuminates the capacious and often overlooked space of possibilities between short stories and novels. Unified by Sarah Evenson's bold and expressive series design, NVLA places works as compact as they are complex in conversation to demonstrate the infinite potential of the form.

WE'RE SAFE WHEN WE'RE ALONE

1

I have lived in the mansion my whole life. I was born here. I have never left. My only glimpse of the outside world is through the windows. There is one in the attic that gives view of the rolling hills in the distance and the forest lining the horizon. There are ponds in the fields surrounding the mansion, and occasionally animals graze on the grass. I have never had the desire to walk across the land. Father has warned me about beauty. That the glorious sky and sweet-smelling flowers are there to lure us. I am a good child. I listen to Father. I will never be tempted to venture outside. I want only what the mansion provides.

In the morning, I wake and brush my teeth. I eat the meal that Father laid out on the table before he left. He is free to come and go. He is an adult. He knows how to face beauty without losing himself in the desire for more. I am lonely most days. This is true. I wish I had a companion to make time pass by more quickly. But loneliness does not make me hunger for the beauty beyond our home. I believe the solution is housed in the confines of the mansion. I have many books to read, songs to practice on the piano, languages to learn. There is always room for the mind to grow. And it is Father who I long for, and every evening he returns, thus solving and ending my condition. I have learned to handle the pain of solitude. It does not drive me to take drastic action. I sit and wait for the unwelcome emotion to pass.

Where Father goes in the morning—I do not know. I have asked, and he chastised me for such curiosity. Knowledge of the world outside the mansion will feed only a longing for it. I must be comfortable with uncertainty, have faith that innocence will bring my life peace. But there are some elements of Father's job I can assume: a part of his work must require him to interact with the beings outside.

They are not really humans. They are figments of a life taking corporeal shape. Ghosts. That is why I have never left the mansion. I am real. I am a person who Father, in his ancient and wondrous way, saved from the brink of death and brought here, to the world in between, where the collector of souls cannot reach me. I have no memory of my life before I was saved. I am too grateful to betray Father by clinging to the past. We are privileged as two humans in a world of myth. This is what Father has told me.

I am not deprived of knowledge. I gain it, not through experience, but through books. Father assigns a new one each week. I read them slowly and learn about the wars, the climates, the cultures. I learn about love and betrayal. Insecurity and jealousy. I learn about nature, how raindrops are formed from vapor. I may have forgotten the details of my past life, but the sensations have stayed with me. When it rains, the mansion shudders and coldness presses itself against my chest. I have an innate understanding of the subjects I am reading, but my memories never come back. The me from that other life is dead. I despise the world outside the mansion. It is an imitation of nature instead of the truth. I must not trust what I see. The ghosts will do anything for me to accept them.

When Father returns home, fear leaves me and I am once again submerged in warmth. I know I am safe. My existence in the mansion makes sense.

Tonight, he takes off his hat and puts down his suitcase. I peel the jacket from his shoulders, which bulge against his cotton shirt. He has grown. I go to close the door, and something sinks within me when I notice how far away Father is, moving up the stairs, his back slumped.

"Wait," I say. "Don't you want to know what I read today?" It is our tradition for me to share what I've read as we saunter through the kitchen, peering into the cupboards to determine what to eat for dinner. We love the classics: *Alice in Wonderland*, Greek myths, *Robinson Crusoe*. We unravel mysteries together. Live in their world for the evening, then return to ours before we sleep. There are not many topics that we discuss. As long as we are near each other, our conversation about the book is enough.

"I'm going to bed early tonight," he says, holding the railing. He tries to smile, but his eyes are heavy and droop.

The cause must be his work. I feel trapped by the weight of my curiosity. "Can you tell me what's bothering you?" I ask.

He pauses, then says, "Nothing's wrong. I haven't been sleeping well."

"I'll make some tea," I say.

"Thank you," he says.

His mind is focused on something beyond the mansion. The outside world intrudes, widening, unwieldy like a piece of furniture that I cannot move but must maneuver around. Whenever weariness overtakes him, I am reminded of how the loneliness of my days does not fully subside when he arrives home. I have to wait longer for Father to truly return. He is still caught up in the outside world. The ghosts are strong, and as he ages his will to resist them weakens. How much longer until he is unable to separate himself from them? Perhaps the solution is for him to stay in the mansion forever like me. But even I can sense the imbalance that this would cause. Somehow, his work stabilizes this world. His presence prevents the ghosts from rampaging. One of us must have knowledge through experience.

2

"Lately, I've been overcome with doubt," Father says. We are in the attic, gazing through the window. The moon is bright, and three cows lap at a pond in the distance. Something is coming our way. I sense an ending. Life as I know it falling apart. Father rocks back and forth in his chair. His heart has made a decision that he can't bring himself to accept. I wish he would go to sleep now, for us to spend the rest of our days in silence. "I fear I've done you a great disservice. You've lived inside these walls all your life. You've never taken a single step outside the door. I'm no longer certain that was the right decision. There is so much you've never seen. So many experiences I've prevented you from having. It's true this world is more treacherous than is apparent to the eye. But it's also true that you are strong enough to withstand it. I should've had more faith in you. I shouldn't have been so afraid. I knew you would suffer if you went out into the world, but that is the only way to grow. You would have found your own path through it, just as I have."

"I'm happy in the mansion," I say.

"Happiness can be a hindrance. It prevents us from changing."

"I don't want to change. I don't care about the outside world."

"Your days will repeat for eternity. I do not want that. I will not always be around. What will you do in this mansion once I'm gone?"

"But you will always be around. I will always have you."

The moon shines through the window. The ghosts are coming. I do not know how much longer the mansion can keep them out. I do not know if Father can protect us.

I hear them. Every night I hear them. Come out, come out, they say. The roof rattles. My bed shakes. Wind pushes against the walls. Their voices are gentle and soft. They can give me what I want. Love, companionship. The emptiness in me echoes. Like a bell, I am struck. I do not give in. I know the promise of love exists only as a tool for deception. They need a soul to fuel their own life. The soul must come willingly. Obedience out of fear taints the act. The illusion of beauty cannot be maintained. The fields shred themselves. I have a mind of my own. I choose solitude. I choose freedom. The ghosts have no control over me.

They mock me for rejecting their kindness. They remind me how flawed and cruel I am. I used to think, But I have Father. Now things have changed. He has changed. If he believes what the ghosts tell him, then I cannot be sure of my own thoughts. I will not admit

I am wrong. Father's voice comes back to me. "I want what's best for you. I've made the wrong decision. It's my fault you have ended up like this."

The worst has come true. A ghost has possessed Father. I have only myself to depend on in this perilous world.

In the morning, I go to the attic. My footsteps are the only noise in the mansion. Father is not awake yet. Not even his snores fill the air. Outside the window, the sun rises above the fields. The sky bloodies with orange and pink and the ghosts appear. They take the form of farmers steering an oxen plow, tilling the land. They are always in some act of nurturing. Simulating innocence without a hint of threat in their actions. I've wondered what they do with the crops, what use their actions have other than maintaining a facade. The ghosts do not need to eat. They cannot experience the pleasures of taste. The extent to which they mimic human behavior borders on devotion. We are their gods.

I will myself to not be afraid of them, even when the farmers stop what they are doing and peer directly at me in the window. They wave. I am chilled. We are far apart and the glass is thick and difficult to see through, but they always know when I am watching them. They always greet me, as though to remind me that I belong with them. I believe their longing for a physical body has given them the ability to sense any human beings nearby. They tighten at the possibility that their wish might be fulfilled. Desperation is what drives them to perform their kindness. The ghosts know that trust is a weapon. When I lose suspicion, they have won. Who is the ghost inside Father? How did they garner his trust? I fight the fear that the ghost is closer to him than I am.

Father is not going to work today. He is wearing his white bathrobe instead of his brown suit. He has not showered, washed his face, or combed his hair. He is in the kitchen, cooking bacon, humming to himself. I ask him what is going on.

"Things have to change," he says. "We have to change how we've been living."

"You have to go to work," I say.

"I'm not needed there anymore. I should be spending more time with you."

I tense up. "Who will do your job?" I ask.

"Someone else will take my place."

"I wish you would go to work. What will you do all day? You'll get bored."

"There's so much to do here. I can renovate the mansion. We can have guests over."

"Guests?"

"Yes, you should meet more people."

"We are the only people here."

"The ghosts are people too," he says. "Things are changing. We have to adapt. We can't resist what is inevitable."

I remain tense. I cannot imagine what these changes will bring. All that is certain is that our way of life is coming to an end. I am not prepared. Everything is changing too quickly: Father's behavior, the safety of the mansion, the arrival of these guests.

The ghosts are free. They have overtaken their keeper. They have convinced Father that coexistence is not only possible but preferable. Peace must exist over control and fear. This is the power of their masterful storytelling. They spin elaborate tales about trauma and retribution. Tales so persuasive that they delude themselves into believing their intentions are innocent. Only in the darkest moments of solitude do they remember the violence they must carry out once they have gained Father's trust. This is what I have learned from my afternoons spent reading books. Stories have taken life inside me, gripped me, squeezed emotions out of my heart that I did not know I was capable of feeling. And those were merely words on a page. A living voice is a thousand times more powerful. The ghosts know the exact sounds that will knock something loose within the listener. They have the tools to carve a space wide enough for the heart to collapse onto itself.

I watch in horror as Father opens the door and commands me not to close it. I feel the wind come inside. The beauty of the rolling hills pours into me. I am overtaken by longing. I want to feel the grass on my palms, taste the air above the bright, clear pond. Already I sense that the mansion will no longer be enough. Desire for the sensual world pulls me away from the place that keeps me safe. I will never be satisfied. Hunger will become my home. Father is wrong. I am not strong. I need to be confined in order to survive.

3

Father is in the yard, cultivating the soil to start a garden. His focus is unbreakable. To my astonishment, soil clings to his hands. Dark and moist. It is real and reacts to his touch. I stand at the door's threshold. He encouraged me to join, but I could smell the ghost inside him and feel its coldness on his breath. Oh, how I wish he would stay inside the mansion. For the boundaries between us and the ghosts to remain firm. I am losing him. And without him, I will have only the mansion.

To all appearances, the world outside has not changed. The rolling hills have not collapsed. The sky has not broken open. The ghosts are too wise to let these projections falter. Whatever promises they have made to Father, they are keeping for now. They are not drunk with freedom. They know that in order to make it last, they must limit themselves. This only deepens my fear of them: I do not know when they will consume us. It is possible that they will allow us to live in peace for such a long period of time that we will begin to believe nothing will ever happen. The only way I can protect Father and our home is to live in fear for the rest of my existence. He is the child now.

For the rest of the day, I fortify the mansion. I hammer nails along the threshold of the front door. I hang sage at the top of the frame. In each room, I wipe down the furniture until the surfaces shine. Each object has a place in the mansion, and I make sure they are exactly where they belong. The canned foods and boxes of cereal in the pantry. The dishes and utensils in the kitchen cabinets and drawers. There is order and things make sense. My surroundings never confuse me. I have purpose and direction.

The outside world, however, is too large to organize. It is not possible for me to know the purpose of each creature's existence. I cannot distinguish what will harm me from what will help me. If I leave, I will be at the mercy of the ghosts. Father has grown tired. He does not want to be in control anymore, the one with knowledge to dispense. His obligation to confront the restless ghosts day after day is a form of entrapment. Instead, Father wants to kneel before a higher power and have it dictate how his life should be. I close my eyes. I imagine the burden that has been on Father for all these years. The loneliness of not having his own father to look to for guidance. Human beings are not meant to be strong on our own. We are meant to serve something else. But I cannot accept the rule of the ghosts. They take me further from the things I love.

After my fortification efforts, I complete my reading for the day. Father calls from the garden. When I reach the door, I see that two ghosts have approached him. They are the farmers from this morning. "Come say hello," Father yells.

I do not respond.

"He's shy," Father says. "He's been in that house all his life. He's never interacted with strangers before. You have to forgive him. He doesn't mean to be rude."

I wish Father would come back inside. I hate his garden. Nothing will grow from this soil. It is all poison. The ghosts wave and smile at me. They have perfected their act. Father accepts a gift from them. A bag of seeds. They help him plant them. They get on their knees and dig through the soil. The three of them work in unison.

"It's getting late," I yell. "We have to start dinner soon."

"You start it, and I'll join you in a moment," Father says.

The ghosts do not say anything. They are focused on the task.

"I don't know what to make. You have to help."

"We'll have a late dinner. I want to finish this first," Father says. "It'll be wonderful. We'll have tomatoes and melons in the summer."

To my relief, the ghosts do not join us for dinner, even after Father invited them. He was insistent, but they said they had chores to finish.

I eat and say the meal is wonderful. Father sighs. He is displeased with how I acted. I do not know if I can act differently in their presence. I ask Father if he notices how clean the mansion is.

"You have to be kinder to them. They're our neighbors. It's important we get along with them."

"I cleaned the entire mansion," I repeat. "Didn't you notice? I worked really hard."

"Of course I noticed. Thank you, but I wish you would do what I ask you to. You'll never know when we'll need their help. We want them to be on our side."

"They're ghosts," I say.

"Yes," Father says.

"You keep referring to them as our neighbors. They're ghosts."

"They're our neighbors too."

"I don't like them."

"You don't have to like them. But you must still treat them with respect. A simple greeting, a smile. It's not difficult."

"I don't want them eating with us."

Father puts down his fork. "I've done you a great disservice. I haven't raised you correctly."

"I'm happy with just the two of us. I don't want to talk to anyone else."

"We can't be alone anymore. We're going to need their help. Things will change very soon."

"No, we're safe as long as we're here," I say. I look around the immaculate room. The mirrors shine. I will continue to put everything in its right place.

"Please, you must listen to me. You have to start seeing the ghosts as real. You have to learn to understand them." Father's face as he says this frightens me. He is so desperate, so genuine in his plea for coexistence. I can see the pain I am causing him, but I also don't know how I can change who I've always been.

For the rest of the night, Father stays in his study, composing letters. He won't tell me what he's writing or who the letters are for. His face is tense with concentration, and the pen scratches loudly against the paper. I walk to the front door and make sure it is closed and locked.

That is when I notice that the nails have been pulled out. There are small holes on the floor. The nails are bent and piled in the trash. The mansion is losing its protection. I place my hand against the wall, hoping to sense its strength. I check the doors of every room to see if they still lock. The window in the attic remains tough and sturdy. When I knock on the glass, the sound is full. I watch clouds drape the moon.

Thunder crashes and lightning splits the sky. It starts to rain, and I know that is a sign. More ghosts are coming from the world of the living. The rain delivers their souls into this world, suffusing the soil with the smell and taste of iron. That is why the sky wails and wails. The rain is so heavy. Many souls are passing over tonight. Many eyes in the world above us are closing forever. I imagine the living asking the souls to come back. Those calls must stay alive inside the ghosts. They are what drives them to drastic action in this world. I hear a dripping sound. I turn around and see that the roof is leaking. The rain is coming in.

Father is no longer in the study. He is nowhere to be found. Thunder reverberates, and the lights in the halls flicker. The wind knocks against the mansion, and the furniture shudders. The stairs groan as I run down them, calling out for Father. His absence meets my gaze in every room. I feel responsible for this. He left because I couldn't agree to change. His clothes are still here. So is his suitcase. I tell myself that nothing is wrong. The worst has not come true. Father is here. He will appear at any moment. I wait for him. More lights start to go out. Darkness consumes the mansion. Rain continues to fall through the roof, pooling on the floor. I am safe. I am not alone.

Noises leak out of the attic. At first, I think it is the storm causing the pipes to groan. But as I approach the room, I am disturbed. It is not the storm at all. I hear wailing and pounding. The floor shakes. I am struck by how fragile the mansion truly is. After all, it is a part of this world, no different from the homes of the ghosts. Except it has to be different. Because Father and I are its inhabitants. The walls yield like flesh. The wooden beams stretch like sinew. Yes, this is my home. I enter the attic, and crouching underneath the window, shadowed by the storm, is a dark figure. An intruder. I am unable to think. My chest is tight. Each breath I take constricts. Instead of running away screaming, I am silent. Fear hushes my body. I approach the figure, sensing something familiar about him. He does not look dangerous. He is naked. His limbs are thin and weak. He can't even push himself up from the floor. I come closer, but his facial features do not become any clearer, even in the burst of a lightning strike. Shadows cling to him like skin-tight clothing. He moans and whimpers. I reach out and lightning strikes again. This time the room turns so bright that I have to shut my eyes. When I open them, the figure is gone. The shadows in the room no longer take a human form. I stand by the window, peering out at the looming hills.

The storm rages. The trees heave under the force of wind and rain. The landscape is torn. But something else, something unnatural, is thrashing in the storm. Darkness. Shadows hungry for souls. Where are the ghosts? Where do they shelter from the madness of this world?

I am drawn away from the window by a pounding at the front door. It is Father. He is shouting my name. I run to let him in. He is completely soaked in his pajamas. His face is stricken. He says that he left the door unlocked, but when he returned, he couldn't get back in. He called me for a long time. Didn't I hear?

I bring Father towels and a change of clothes. We gather around the fireplace. The warmth crawls up his arms. Color returns to his face. He is calm and relaxed now. I ask him why he left the house, and he says he thought he heard someone he recognized.

"Who?" I ask.

"I'm not sure. It was just a feeling I had."

"Did you find him?"

"No. There wasn't anyone there. I don't know what I was thinking."

"You have to stay inside. It's not safe out there."

"I know. It was a mistake."

I force myself not to make assumptions. I tell Father it was probably the wind, or a part of the roof falling off. He nods, and we resume our night as though nothing happened. I am deeply troubled. Strange noises have appeared before, but Father never paid attention to them. I don't know the significance of this voice to him, and I don't want to know. For the rest of the night, we keep busy by cleaning the puddles in the attic. We watch the rain collect in buckets. I keep thinking about the dark figure. I open my mouth to ask Father about what I saw, but then I stop. I am being foolish. I am giving into delusion. What good can come from disturbing the peace? My eyes ache. My mind spirals. Stop it. There was no man. There is only Father, and his love for me.

Father tucks me into bed. I melt into the sheets. We listen to thunder. He stares up at the roof, his eyes moving as though he's tracking some entity prowling above us. Father takes a deep breath and says, "I have something I want you to do." He grasps my right hand. "Now close your eyes and tell me what you see."

"I don't understand. What do you mean? What should I see?"

"Just try," Father commands.

I close my eyes. Father's hold on my hand tightens.

"What do you see?" he asks.

"Nothing," I say.

"Focus."

I hear thunder. I see darkness and rain. My breathing turns ragged. "There's nothing," I say. "I don't see anything."

"No, it's there. Our memory. You're not trying hard enough."

Father squeezes his palms, and I wince. I say, "You're hurting me."

He lets go. Blood rushes back to my hand, and my skin stings. I open my eyes, and I see Father sitting on the edge of the bed, his back slumped, his face buried in his palms.

Thunder cracks, and then the rain stops. There's no longer pattering on the roof. Only silence visits us in the room.

4

Father spends the next day on the roof patching up the leaks. Once he starts, he discovers more and more. I am afraid of heights. I stand in the attic and track the sounds his footsteps make across the roof. I hope it is strong enough to hold him. I hope he is watching his step. The fall would cause irreversible harm. That would be the only reason for me to leave the mansion, to save Father.

I walk down to the front door to see if anyone appears in the field. I keep expecting a ghost to come and convince Father to return to work. But his absence seems to make no difference. It is hard for me to imagine that Father is not needed wherever he used to go. This world continues to move forward without us.

The rain has dislodged the seeds from the garden. They float in puddles over the soil. All of Father's work from yesterday has gone to waste. He will replant them once he is done with the roof. I don't understand why he even bothers. He should spend time with me, working inside the mansion, fortifying it against the weather.

The fields and rolling hills are radiant. Last night's rain has strengthened their beauty. The grass is a deeper shade of green. The ponds glisten like crystals. The two ghosts from yesterday arrive on our yard. They ask Father if he would like some help. The storm damaged their farm too. At the front door, I watch them climb the ladder. I am cold all over. My desire to leave the mansion grows. Father needs me to protect him. There is only one of him, and two of them. I run back to the attic and listen to them work. One ghost points out the mistakes Father has made, and shows him a better way to patch a leak. Father thanks them, says he couldn't have finished this in time without them. He again invites them for dinner as repayment. They refuse, saying again that they have too many chores.

After they leave, Father climbs down from the roof. All he can talk about is how kind the ghosts are, how pleasant they are to talk to, how knowledgeable they are about the objects in this world. He pours lemonade for himself and wipes the sweat from his face with a hand towel. I've never seen him this happy before, not even when we were discussing a book we both loved.

I look through the cupboards and ask him what he'd like to eat, but he is not listening. He says I have to give the ghosts a chance, that he can feel our lives changing for the better if we embrace them, if I learn to go outside the mansion.

I say I am hungry, that I need to eat before I can talk. Father is silent. Then his eyes widen. He opens the fridge and pulls out a shepherd's pie. "They gave it to me. They said they made too much food, and thought we would like some." Father reheats the pie in the oven and then places it on the table. The crust is golden. The meat and vegetables look decadent and hearty. I gulp. I have a hard time resisting. Instead I eat toast with slices of ham as Father swallows spoonful after spoonful of the pie.

"You have to try some," Father says. "It's absolutely wonderful." His satisfaction repulses me. The way his cheeks bulge. The way he coughs from swallowing too fast. The chunks of food that fall out of his mouth. It is clear the ghosts have put an enchantment on the pie, and Father doesn't even realize it.

"Stop eating," I say. "You should save room for dessert."

"What do we have?"

"Let me find some."

As I search, Father continues to eat.

"You have to try the food the ghosts made," Father repeats, this time more sternly, as though there will be punishment if I refuse. This tone chills me and I sit back down. I watch as he cuts into the pie and then puts the plate in front of me. "You have to trust me," he says. "It's delicious. You won't regret eating it."

I nod. I push the fork into the filling. The crust is damp. Steam rises from the wet chunks of meat.

"They put a lot of work and care into baking this pie. It's not right to let it go to waste."

I nod and slowly chew.

"How is it?"

"It's delicious," I say.

"It's perfectly seasoned. Not too salty, not too bland. Very warm and filling."

"Yes, I agree," I say.

"Now, I want you to close your eyes," Father says.

"Why?"

"Close your eyes and tell me what you see when you eat the pie."

Frustration mounts. I don't want to play this game anymore, but Father's face is so serious, as though this is somehow a matter of life and death. My curiosity is becoming too much to handle. I don't need to venture outside to be confronted with questions and confusion. Father is bringing the unknown right into the mansion. I close my eyes. I tell him I see nothing.

"Take this seriously," Father says.

"What am I supposed to see?"

"The ghosts. Their memories."

"Why would I see that? They're not real."

"Focus on the food they made. That's real. What you taste, how it satisfies your hunger. All of that is real."

"I'm full," I say, and I open my eyes. "I can't eat anymore."

Father doesn't take the plate away. He leaves the uneaten food on the table. He leaves it there to rot.

Our supplies will dwindle. Whenever Father returned from work, he brought home groceries, toiletries, and anything else we might need. I am not sure when he intends to do this now. We will run out of food in less than a week. We have already used up the shampoo and body wash. I believe this is all a part of Father's plan to drive me out of the mansion. Eventually, I'll have to go out on my own to find food. I can't stand this thought. Entering the world out of force and necessity instead of my own choice. I am determined to ration our food and make it last for as long as possible. The shepherd's pie lies half-eaten and covered on the table. If it comes down to it, I'll accept more food from the ghosts. More than likely, they'll continue to make offerings. But I'll eat only enough to fend off the pangs of hunger. I will not give in. I will not give in.

I beg Father to come to the library with me, to read a book out loud and fill the mansion with his voice. But he says that we must put away the books for now. The worlds they conjure distance us from reality. They fill us with voices that we should not listen to. I wrap my arms tightly around the book I want Father to read as he puts on his boots and gloves. He says he has to work on the garden if he wants the tomatoes to bloom this season. He has to keep his hands busy so his mind does not wander. He kneels in the moist soil, and I have the sense that he is sinking into the earth.

During the week, I do everything I can to keep Father inside the mansion. I clog the toilets and the sinks with wads of paper. I break a step on the stairs. I complain that the heater does not come on at night, that I am always too cold here.

As soon as Father fixes something, I point out another issue, and another. But I can never keep him inside for long. Each day seems endless. He always has enough time to go outside, work on his garden, and chat with the ghosts.

They ingratiate themselves into his life more and more. They walk him through the fields. They teach him the complicated methods of their farmwork. Father helps them feed the livestock, clean the pigs' pen and horses' stable. I don't understand his fascination with the ghosts. I don't understand how he can quit his job to grow wheat and clean smelly animals. He no longer cares about books, about knowledge of politics or history. All he talks about during dinner is the lives of the ghosts. He describes for me how happy and fulfilled they are. It is all an act, I want to tell him. They have fooled you. This life is not enough for them. They want more. They want what we have. And then I wonder to myself, What is it that we have?

I have never been more alone.

As a desperate measure, I decide to inflict harm onto myself. It is a decision that I struggle with for days. I am not immune to pain. I am terribly fearful of it, especially when I know that it is coming. The stress of anticipation drains me. In order to force Father to stay by my side, the injury has to be drastic. It cannot be a mere cut or bruise, something that he can put a bandage over before resuming his life on the outside. But I can't go too far. I don't want to risk losing my body. I don't want to risk crossing over to the other side.

One afternoon, as I walk down the stairs, I hurl myself off them, making sure to fall onto my shoulders to protect my head. The noise of the impact is enough to draw Father back into the mansion. His response is exactly what I want. Even with the pain, I struggle to suppress my smile, the sheer joy that comes from witnessing Father's devotion.

He carries me to the sofa. He examines my body. Nothing is broken, but I complain about a headache. He rubs medicinal oil on my limbs, and brings out my favorite treat, chocolate chip cookies. I ask him to read to me, and this time he gladly agrees.

We spend the following days reading book after book. To my delight, he is more watchful of me. He stays by my side to make sure I don't trip on the stairs again, that I don't burn myself while cooking. He says he is afraid to go outside and leave me unaccompanied.

Then the unexpected happens: Father invites the ghosts to watch over me. This way he can work in the garden and go into town and buy the medicine I need. Panic fills me to the point that I forget to breathe. I don't say anything in response to his announcement of this plan.

"They'll know how to take care of you," Father says. "I trust them. They want only to live with us in peace."

"I'm better now," I say. "I can take care of myself. They don't need to come."

"What if something happens? If they're here, one of them can head into town and alert me."

"No, no, no," I say.

Father clasps my face and smiles down at me. "You'll see. Things are changing. We'll have a different life soon."

5

When the ghosts arrive, I act as if they are not there.

To my horror, they cross the door's threshold with ease. Nothing can keep them out. They have always been able to go in and out with ease. I wonder how often they have roamed the mansion and peeked into my room unnoticed. It is possible that they can turn invisible to my eyes whenever they want.

Their faces are alive with concern. It sickens me how they squat next to the sofa and check my head for a fever, how they stock the pantry with food and supplies to help me get better.

"It's not right," they say. "It's not healthy for a child to stay in the house all day. You have to play outside and get plenty of sunshine like the other children in the town."

I stare up at the ceiling. I cannot hear them.

"Look at how pale you are," the ghosts say. "No wonder you got sick and injured. Your bones must be so weak. You need to play in order to grow. Tell us. What can we do for you?"

One ghost starts cooking dinner. I realize they're contaminating all of our food and every surface of the mansion with their touch. Even after they leave, I'll still feel them around me, inside of me.

The other ghost walks up and down the stairs. "These steps will break at any moment. They're so flimsy. How old is this house? The air is awfully stale and musty. Everything needs to be fixed up. We can do that for you. Your father must be very busy. He doesn't have time to fix every inch of this house. You're bound to get hurt more often. It isn't safe!"

I close my eyes. I am falling asleep. Soon Father will be back, and the ghosts will be gone.

"There, there," they say, stroking my hair. "You'll get better soon. You'll heal up. We'll make sure of it."

Their hands are cold and slimy. I can't believe that they're able to touch me. That their bodies have weight and mass.

"What do you want?" I finally say.

"What do we want?" they reply.

"Whatever it is, just don't hurt Father. Leave him alone."

"We want to be good neighbors," they say. "We want you to be a part of our community."

As they stroke my face, I feel as though they are taking a part of me with them.

When I wake, Father has returned.

"You shouldn't have invited them," I say. "They touched everything in the mansion. We're not safe from them anymore."

Father grabs a bottle of pills out of a plastic bag. "They said they had a wonderful time taking care of you. They said you're a good child and that they hope they can see you again."

I turn my face away when he hands me the pills.

"Take them, you'll feel better," he says.

I groan. I toss and turn.

Father snatches my chin and holds me still. He drops the pills into my mouth, and presses a glass of water to my lips.

I drink.

"You can't trust them," I say, even though at this point I know how futile my words are. But I hope that by voicing them into the air, I am casting a spell. I am reaching the part of Father that I used to know. That the ghosts have locked away. "Can you promise me that you won't leave again?"

"I left to get you medicine," he says.

"We have everything we need in the mansion."

"That isn't true. Do you want to know what it's like in the town? It's wonderful. There are markets, shops, and restaurants, and children playing all around. Life there is bright and vibrant. You could have had so many friends if I'd encouraged you to leave. You wouldn't have been afraid like you are now. The townspeople—"

"They're ghosts."

"The townspeople treated me kindly. They guided me to the pharmacy. They expressed great concern for you. They even lent me money to buy you this medicine."

"I'll never go there. I don't ever want to talk to the ghosts."

"Things are changing. We have to change too. The town can provide for you in ways I can't."

"Oh, Father, you're all I need. I don't want anybody else."

Fear rises to the surface of Father's face. Life with me is not enough for him. I am alone. I have no one. He wants to give up his responsibility of me. He is tired of this world, just like the ghosts are. He wants to move on, whether to the land of the living or the land of the dead, I do not know.

Soon, I realize that the ghosts have not left the house.

After Father feeds me the medicine, I hear a commotion in the kitchen. Father has a strange expression on his face, a mix between doubt and guilt. He is hiding something. He must have a reason, otherwise I can't understand why he would place me in this dark, murky world of the unknown.

Father brings the ghosts back to the living room.

They hold their heads down. They appear solemn and mournful. The round shape of their eyes, the curves of their noses and lips. No, no, they're not here, they're not real.

"What did you put in the medicine?" I ask Father.

"Nothing. It's for the pain you feel."

"You put something in the medicine. Why do the ghosts look so different?"

"You're seeing more clearly," Father says. "That's normal, that's how it should be. You should see them like how I see them."

"Something's wrong with me. I don't want your medicine."

"You're afraid," the wife says. "It's OK, I understand. You don't have to be. We're not here to hurt you."

She sits next to me on the sofa, and the husband stands back. He keeps his distance. He seems to sense my hatred and doesn't want to provoke me. He knows his place in this world. He knows that ghosts and humans should not interact.

"We should go. We've stayed for long enough. Let him rest," the husband says.

The wife glances at Father, and he shakes his head. She tenses her jaw. Her eyes shift in their sockets. She forces a smile. "I'm sorry," she says to Father, "but I don't think I can wait anymore. I've been patient enough, don't you think? We've all been very patient since you stopped your work."

Father says, "You've been doing so well. I know what I promised, but he's not ready."

"We have to try," the wife says. "It doesn't hurt to try right now. I just want to see them again." She holds out her hand at me.

I am frozen. Tell them to go away, I think. Tell them to leave us alone. But Father doesn't say anything. His eyes are unblinking.

"Take my hand," the wife says, "and tell me what you see." Her hands are tanned and rough from the work on the farm. Dirt lines her fingernails.

"Son, listen to her."

This is it, I think. This is the moment the ghost will possess me. She has fooled Father with a story that I do not know about. She has convinced him that she is innocent so that she can take over my body and soul. She holds out her hand, and I feel as though I have no other option. Father is watching me.

I close my eyes.

Silence fills the air. After some time, the wife says, "It's not working. He doesn't see anything. I can sense it."

"I'm sorry," Father says. "The time will come when this world will return to its rightful order. He just needs more time."

When I open my eyes, I am still myself. I have complete control.

Her hand slides out of my hold. She stands up. The expression on her face is unbearably sad. The husband comforts her as they make their way to the door. Father bids them farewell, and the wife smiles at me before she leaves. This time it doesn't seem forced. I touch my face, my chest. This body, with all its flaws, is still mine. It is not so easy for the ghosts to possess us, if it is even possible for them to.

6

More ghosts appear in the fields. The harvest season is coming, Father tells me. The ghosts need extra help to reap the grain. From the attic window, I see ghosts swinging scythes, ghosts leading oxen across the land. I see children running through the wheat stalks, giggling and yelling.

There is so much life in the outside world now. I can watch all day and never get bored. There is always something to notice. How have the ghosts learned to live such fulfilling lives? Can it really be an act? How much better can the world of the living be for them to want to give up all of this? Perhaps in the process of myth-making, something real and alive forms for them.

Father, of course, is among them, performing a different role each day. He wakes up excited by possibility. He learns the names of all the plants. He plays with the ghost children. He swims in the pond with the farmers after a long day of work. I imagine that the work he engaged in before this was lifeless. That it isolated him to the point of numbness, overwhelmed by responsibility. It seems the goal of all life is to return to the state of the child, when we are most apt for learning, and the world is new and wondrous. He has given up so much power, so much knowledge.

I am stubborn, and stay firm within my routine in the mansion. But longing is slowly morphing into anguish. The beauty of the outside world tempts me. I start to find the books in the library boring and lifeless. There is nothing left in the mansion for me to fix. I gaze out the window more often, imagining what it would feel like to run through the wheat stalks, chasing after another child.

Father is fixated. In all our conversations, he is desperate to talk about a ghost who feels familiar to him. He has no clear memories of this ghost, but he is certain they've met before and bonded deeply during a time of misfortune. During our meals, he describes the ghost's complexion, physical features, clothes, and mannerisms.

Apparently, his appearance is similar to ours: brown skin, dark hair, a wide, square face. Father has talked only briefly to this ghost. He feels too shy and intimidated in his presence. The ghost is quiet, and in gatherings he simply nods and chuckles in response to the conversation. There doesn't seem to be anything particularly distinctive about him. He is one of the farmers who drives the oxen plow. He works hard and never complains. It is the ghost's normalcy that drives Father close to madness. He can't understand why something inside him brightens whenever he is in the presence of this ghost.

I hate listening to Father ramble on. I cannot help but feel intense jealousy toward this ghost. What exactly is the key to Father's affection? I used to be able to elicit his attention without even trying. But now, no matter what I do, his eyes look right past me.

I watch the ghosts in the fields through the attic window for days. I pay special attention to the ghost Father follows around. Father is wrong. There is something peculiar about this ghost. Whenever they gather in a group to take a break from their work and share food someone has made, the ghost stands outside of the circle. He does not feign the enthusiasm that I witness in so many of the other ghosts. Their sickening laughter, the way they throw their heads back and open their mouths wide enough to swallow the entire sky. He is focused only on work. He does not cajole Father into joining their world. I have the impression that he would prefer for us to stay in the mansion, for humans and ghosts to stay separate.

I grow more and more tired of watching from afar while the ghosts and Father create a life together. I can't focus on reading my books because their laughter and the children's yells distract me.

I clean the mansion, but the staleness in the air only grows until I am constantly coughing. Mold spots spread along the walls. The rain did much more damage than I thought. The more alone I become, the slower time seems to pass. The repetition of my actions brings me little solace. I am astonished by how necessary conversations and companionship are. I imagine the horror of spending the rest of eternity sitting completely still, staring at a single view. The mansion is becoming a source of madness. I can't bear to be in its rooms. To look at its walls.

One afternoon, as I try to read on the sofa, an odd sound jolts me out of concentration. It is not the ghosts outside. It is coming from the attic. I stare up at the ceiling, and walk toward the stairs. It sounds as though someone is dragging metal chains across the floor. Something in my heart aches and whispers at me to follow the sound. But when I reach the attic, there's nothing unusual. There are no chains. I wander the room and run my fingers along the walls, peering at the cracks and grooves. I've been here so often, but do I really know this tucked-away space? I freeze, then jerk my head toward the window. The sound has come back. The source is out of sight, and yet it is so loud that if I reach out into the air, I think I might squeeze my fingers around the chains. I stand at the window. Fog has covered the landscape. Shadowy figures haunt the air. They must be the ghosts, continuing their farmwork at a strange hour. But there are other dark shapes that I don't recognize. Monstrous and taller than any tree, lacking any resemblance to the natural world.

A man runs out of the fog. He stops, and looks back at the landscape. He pulls at his hair, and buckles over in pain. Sunshine pierces the fog behind him, and the man turns. He screams at the dark shapes. He runs back to them, and is lost in the emptiness.

I rush down the stairs. I tear the front door open. I am prepared to yell as loudly as I can for him to return, and take shelter in the mansion. But when I stand at the threshold, I see that the fog is gone. The sky is bright blue, and the sun shines warmly. The farmland and the rolling hills are radiant. The ghosts are hard at work, calmly going about their day. The only dark shapes are the shadows that they cast, thin and innocent.

I rub my eyes. I rub them until I am sure I can see clearly.

The day comes when I give in to temptation. I let my hunger draw me away from the attic window. I will see the mysteries of the outside world undistorted.

As soon as I take a step onto the lawn, I am startled by how soft the ground is compared to the mansion floor. My shoe sinks, and I almost lose my balance. I stand still and feel the air wrap me in its warmth. The flowers and leaves sway before me. I gaze at the openness of the sky and am dizzied by its endlessness. The sun burns me. How is my body affected so deeply by an imitation? Is my body unable to distinguish between what is real and what is false? Why would the ghosts even desire a body like mine?

Father lifts his head up from the field, and waves ecstatically. He is working on the land as always. I smile. It has been so long since he's reacted this way to my presence. He embraces me and expresses how proud he is. He is not someone who gives in to fear and runs away.

"You won't regret this," he says. "You've made the right choice. It'll be tough at first, but then you'll see how free you can be."

Father is gripping my shoulders so hard that I have to suppress my pain. I nod and force myself to return his enthusiasm. He grabs my hand and leads me further into the outside world, past the wheat fields and rows of newly planted seeds. He introduces me to the ghosts he is friends with. Their smiles disturb me. They hold out their hands, and I am stiff and cold as I shake them one after another.

Already I long for the safety of the mansion, the enclosure of its thick walls. Out here it is alarmingly easy to get lost. If I lose sight of Father, I'll lose the strength to find my way back to the mansion.

"What a handsome child you are!" the ghosts say. "You look just like your father. So strong, so lively. We've heard you are afraid of us. But what is there to be afraid of? We are all very friendly. You'll soon find that you like being with us more than you think. We have everything you can want. Whatever you want to do, just tell us, and we'll find the proper role for you among us."

The ghosts pinch my face and coo at me. They lift me onto their shoulders. They give me high fives, and teach me to ride an ox. I feel nauseous and uncertain. Even with someone beside the ox to keep it calm, I worry I'll fall off at any moment. I am drained of energy, and have no desire to do anything but what Father tells me. Already my life in the mansion seems distant.

I catch sight of Father and his friend. They're standing apart from the group, deep in their own conversation. Father appears grave. His usual mask of hopefulness has cracked. His friend is calm as always. I sneak toward them and eavesdrop.

"You've lost your abilities. It's no use to continue trying. You can't keep pretending that this world will stay as it is."

"I'm not. I know things are about to change. But there must be a solution. I am close to finding it. My son is almost ready."

Before I can hear any more of their conversation, the other ghosts find me and pull me back into their group.

They leave me on a playground with the rest of the children. The children display the same unbridled enthusiasm as their parents. They act as though they've known me for a long time. As though there is no difference between our existences.

I am afraid of their friendliness. I don't know what I've done to cause it. I don't know if I'll do something to make them change how they feel. A few of them whisper to one another, and then start laughing. I believe they are glancing at me as they laugh. I stand, unblinking. I wonder what I look like to them, if there is something funny on my face. The others are going down the slide or pushing off on the swings.

Someone grabs my hand, and shouts, "Tag, you're it!" They're running in a frenzy. I run left, then stop, then run right. I don't know who to go to, what to do. Everyone is too fast. Each time I reach someone, they escape my grasp, and I am left panting.

"Come on!" the ghosts scream. "You can do better than that. Are you already tired?"

My legs are sore. My lungs burn. "I'm fine," I say. "I can keep going."

"You're too slow! You'll never catch us."

Their laughter has only increased in volume. Their energy seems exponential. The source of their glee is a deep mystery to me. I grow dizzy. I stop completely, and the ghosts seem not to notice. They continue to play as though I was never even a part of the game. I feel as though I am still standing in the attic, watching the scene through a window. The ghosts appear to share a clear understanding of how they should behave in this world. They do not seem to doubt who they are or what role they have among one another.

I stand on the edge of the playground. I am afraid to move. Father is nowhere in sight. The fields and rolling hills rise in front of me. I wait for someone to notice that I am lost and guide me out of this place.

7

That evening Father comments on the transformation I've made. He's been worried that I would stay in the attic forever, all alone. But now I have the opportunity to change, for my spirit to become more open and inviting. The ghosts even told him that I was a joy to have around. The children loved playing tag with me and hoped I would come back tomorrow. I find it difficult to breathe. I grip my fork and stare at my plate and force myself to smile.

"I had a fun time too," I say.

"I knew it," Father says. "I knew if you just gave them a chance, things would work out."

"You're right," I say.

"I'm so relieved. You have all these friends you can play with. You don't have to be inside all day. They can teach you all sorts of things that I can't."

"I hope I get to know them better," I say.

"You will," Father says. "You can start helping me with my work soon. I'm glad I can share this part of my life with you now."

His excitement feels genuine. I am moved by his words. I can't bring myself to disrupt this mood we're in. For the first time in weeks, the air in the mansion is light, and I try to enjoy the fresh shepherd's pie that the ghosts made.

For most of the next day, I am able to stay by Father's side. In the field, I help him harvest the wheat. Later we feed the animals in their pens. Our time together has the same quality as the old days in the mansion. I feel the intimacy we shared over books and housekeeping. I expect this to last, but eventually Father wanders off to complete his own tasks.

Before he leaves, I ask if I can come with him, and he is adamant that I spend time on my own.

"Where are you going?"

He doesn't answer. Fear ages his face. He stares at the fog on the horizon and rubs his head in pain.

"Is it your job? Are you going back to work?"

"No. I will tell you soon."

"Tell me now."

"I don't want you to be afraid."

"Of what? The ghosts are threatening you, aren't they? Let me help you."

Father shakes his head. He says he'll find me by dinner time. I watch him disappear over a hill.

As soon as he is gone, ghosts start to run up the hill in a panic, glancing over their shoulders as though something is following them. Father is not among them. They pay no attention to me as they race past. These ghosts have no mask of cheerfulness. They don't pretend that I am a frightened child.

I am about to go search for Father when a ghost from the farm grabs my arm and leads me to the playground. I have the terrifying sense that this one has been watching me the whole day, awaiting a moment when I'm alone. The sky feels full of eyes. I stand in the playground surrounded by the children.

"I don't want to play," I say.

"Come to this side," half of them say. They've formed two lines. "You're on our team."

"I'm not going anywhere. I'm staying here until Father finds me."

"He's busy. The adults have things to do."

"He'll come for me soon. I don't have time to play."

"We're playing Red Rover. Come on, you'll really like it. Just try, please."

Before I can respond, two ghosts grab each of my arms and pull me to their line. I am startled by how strong they are. My strength is almost nonexistent in comparison. They ask me if I know how to play. I recall reading about the game in one of my books. I will not enjoy this. I do not understand how anyone can think this game is fun.

A ghost from the other line steps out and charges forward. He does not break our line, but I still buckle from the reverberations of his impact. Then it is someone's turn from our line to charge forward. She manages to break the other line, and the ghosts erupt into a fit of laughter. Two new ghosts join our line, and we resume this pattern, which seems to go on forever.

To my horror a ghost charges right at me, and I feel myself shrinking in response. I pull away, but the ghosts in my line tighten their grip and hold me still.

"Stop," I say. He crashes. I fly backward but don't break my hold. Once I manage to find my footing, I realize that they are cheering me on. Then one ghost after another charges into me, hurling me into the air, and yet the other ghosts won't let me break my hold. I say I can't play any longer, but they do not hear. They continue to hold me in line. My body grows weaker and weaker. It is bruised and tender. My head swirls with dizziness. But they continue to slam into me. Soon enough I lose the will to speak.

"Don't be afraid," they say. "Learn to be strong like us."

I want Father, I think. And the ghosts laugh and laugh.

When Father sees me on the lawn, he is troubled. He examines my face and arms. "What happened? What did you do to yourself?"

I am too dizzy to respond.

The ghosts tell him about Red Rover. How I insisted on playing even after I got injured.

Father sighs and shakes his head.

The haze in my mind is dense and heavy. I don't know how to explain myself.

"We told him to stop," the ghosts say. "But he was having so much fun, he didn't care."

"Is that true?" Father asks.

I feel like screaming.

"We tried to tell him how dangerous it was. But he wouldn't listen. He wasn't worried at all," the ghosts say.

"They're lying," I whisper.

Father furrows his brow. He lightly touches a bruise on my shoulder.

"We'll try harder to stop him next time. We were all so scared. Someone could have really gotten hurt."

"You have to be strong," Father says. "You have to force them to stop when they are out of line. You have that ability."

The ghosts say, "He was having fun, he liked the game."

Father glares at them.

The ghosts lose their smiles. They turn shy and serious. "We didn't mean to cause any harm. We were just playing around."

"I didn't want to play," I say. "I asked them to stop."

"That's not enough," Father says. "You have to be stronger. You can't be scared of them."

"We just wanted to play," the ghosts say. "We thought he was having fun."

Father says, "Do you hear me?"

I stiffen. I say, "Where did you go?"

"I had to take care of business. I am doing everything I can to protect you."

"No, you left."

"The ghosts were calling. I had to help them."

"I was calling to you too. Did you hear me?"

"You're not powerless," he says. "You have to start being strong."

I put my palm over a bruise and stand completely still as I press down on it.

Father acts more gently for the rest of the evening. He cooks pot roast and gives me medicine. We sit on the sofa as he reads a fairy tale out loud. I have all of his attention again, but this time I am not moved by it. I feel cold all over, and I long to be alone, deep within my anger. He asks what's wrong, and I say nothing. I wonder what I can do to bring myself solace, who I can go to. Even in the mansion, I am no longer safe.

"Is this about those children?" Father says. "I'll talk to them again first thing in the morning."

"They're ghosts. I shouldn't be playing with them," I say.

Father is hardly recognizable. His words always have some motive behind them.

"You must understand how important it is for you to get along with them. We need them to survive."

"I don't care what we need. I hate them."

"They're not what you think. They can be kind too."

"No, I'm not leaving the mansion anymore," I say.

"Give it time. You're new to them. They're testing your boundaries. They'll tease you at first, but then they'll see you as one of their own. You have to give them a chance."

Father's eyes shine. His determination scares me. Why does he want to believe in the ghosts this much? I stand up and leave the living room.

He follows me. I hear his footsteps in the hall, the drum of his breath. He is coming closer and closer.

"Stop it," I shout.

"Where are you going? Just let me talk to you."

I've had enough talk. I want silence. I want to live far away on a remote island like Robinson Crusoe. All I would have to worry about is finding shelter from the rain and where in the ocean I can hunt for fish. No one will bother me. I can gaze at the sky in peace. Crusoe's fear was never that he would not be able to leave the island, but that someone would force him back into the world to live among people.

"Leave me alone," I say. I've locked the attic door. Father stands on the other side, knocking and knocking. His voice can't reach me anymore. It enters my ears, but it does not move anything inside me. I stand in front of the window and gaze out at the world, no longer a part of it. This is true happiness, when I am safe from hunger.

The ghosts have been busy. There are houses growing on the rolling hills. They have settled right next to us.

The houses are in different stages of construction. Some are half built, some are merely skeletons of wood and metal. A few are completely done. They are modest. Their windows glow with the light from oil lamps. I can see their shadows moving inside. They are trying to put their children to sleep. There is laughter in their homes. There is always laughter. No one is ever weeping or mournful. Is it because they have already died once? Does death imprison you in everlasting joy? I feel pity for them. Forced to behave in one manner for eternity, smiling indiscriminately at everything. They are dishonest. They'll never know what brings them true happiness. But it is not like I am any different. Their life is my future.

8

Now that I will not come to them, the ghosts come to me. Father is busy helping to build their houses. New crops grow in the fields, no longer requiring their creators' constant assistance. They've found a way to exist on their own.

I stop watching the ghosts from the attic. I fall deeper into my world of books. The characters demand so little of me. I can study their lives in safety. But still, the loud laughter of the ghosts reminds me of their existence. The outside world intrudes through my ears.

I am reading in the living room when the children knock on the front door. I do not open it. "We have a new game today," they shout. "We think you'll really like it."

I push a chair against the door. I place my whole weight onto it.

"We're sorry about yesterday. We only wanted you to have fun."

How many of them are out there? Their voices are so loud that the door trembles.

"The adults told us to be nicer. We won't do anything to hurt you. We really do feel bad about yesterday. We haven't had a new friend in a long time. Please join us. We want you to be a part of us."

Where is Father? Does he see what they're doing?

I close my eyes. I know with terrible certainty that Father will not come and order the children to go away. He is lost in his work for the ghosts. He will not return to the mansion until evening.

"Let us in. We need the mansion to play the game. Do you want to know what it is? It's hide-and-seek. Your house is the best place for it. There are so many areas to hide. It'll be so much fun. No one can get hurt. We promise we'll find you."

I run out of the living room. I can't escape.

At the end of the hall stands a dark figure. No eyes, no mouth. A living shadow. The figure falls onto his knees. He buckles over and curls into a fetal position. He isn't a ghost. He isn't one of the children. Who could have let him in? I break out of my debilitating fear, and I run up the stairs. I lock myself in a bathroom. I stuff my ears with cotton balls. To my surprise, I can't hear the children at all. I've found relief from them in here. Nothing can disturb me. I fall asleep soothed.

When I wake up, I take out the cotton balls, and am relieved to hear that the mansion is silent. In the bathroom, I wash my face and take a short shower. No dark figure meets me when I descend the stairs and turn the corner. I go to the kitchen where Father sits with a group of children.

They all turn to greet me. They flash identical smiles, with their teeth showing and a glint in their eyes.

"Where have you been?" Father asks. "Come eat with the other children."

There are plates of cookies and pastries on the table.

"Why did you let them in?" I ask.

"I didn't. They were already here when I got home."

I turn to look at the hall.

"They were hungry from playing all day. They said they asked you to play with them."

"I didn't hear them," I say. "I was sleeping."

"Do you feel better after resting?" the ghosts say.

I don't answer them.

"Well that's very kind of you all." Father turns to me. "Isn't it nice of them to make an effort to include you?"

"He must have been really tired when we asked. We understand. We can play together another time."

"There's still time left in the day. Why don't you all play now?" Father says.

I stare at the bright red jam on the pastries. They glisten like jewels. I want to shove them down Father's throat until he chokes. I want to be strong enough to grab the ghosts and hurl them out of the mansion.

The ghosts shake their heads. "Oh no, it's getting late. We're sure that he doesn't want to play right now. We understand. We'd rather play when he feels better."

"Well, that's thoughtful of you all. Isn't that thoughtful?" Father asks me.

"I don't like strawberry jam," I say. "I don't want to eat that."

"I can bring you something else. What would you like?"

"We love strawberry jam," the ghosts shout. "Thank you for the food." All at once they reach for pastries. They eat voraciously, the jam clinging to their lips. I see the crumbs mix with their saliva, the jam swirling around their tongues, strings of it pulled apart by their teeth.

I do not feel hungry tonight. I will not eat a single thing Father cooks. He no longer listens. Anything I tell him, he quickly dismisses, and then he disappears among the ghosts.

The next day, I find that the front door is open, and no matter how hard I pull the doorknob, it won't stay closed. Father has done something to it. I examine every inch of the frame and can't figure out how he accomplished this. Now there is nothing to keep the children out.

Already, along the horizon, a line of them appears, each one holding the hand of the child in front of them. They swing their arms as they prance down the hill and sing a nursery rhyme. The sun shines mercilessly behind them.

I am furious. I am tired of running away and hiding from them. I sit in the kitchen and eat my breakfast and start building an invisible barrier around myself.

Nothing they say or do will bother me. I will carry on with my routine as though I am the only person in existence.

When the ghosts arrive, they greet me enthusiastically. My barrier falters immediately as one after another they pull me into their chests and hug me. The succession is endless. I am embraced for so long that I grow intensely weary and dizzy. Before I can recover from one hug, the ghost behind them tackles me into another embrace. They start to blur into one another. It is as though as soon as they finish their hug, they move to the back of the line so they can continue the assault forever.

I think, I am human. I am a human being. They cannot hurt me. They cannot possess me. But then their embraces do something strange to me. Visions surge through my mind. Sunlight, a field, a child being held, a child being kissed on the cheek. It is their birthday. It is Christmas. The images flash like a reel of memories. But I know they are not mine. I have not experienced any of these events. They are memories of the children when they were alive.

When I can no longer think clearly, when my consciousness has melted into a watery mess, the ghosts stop. They ask me what they can eat for breakfast. I say I don't know. They open every cupboard in the kitchen. They pull out cans and boxes of food. They eat handfuls of cereal and fruit drenched in syrup. Crumbs fall from the boxes and scatter across the floor.

"You have to invite us over more often," they shout. "Your place is wonderful. What else is there?"

They invade the other rooms in the mansion. They pull out drawers and throw clothes onto the floor. They play tag around the furniture, leaving prints of dirt on the couch. Screams and laughter fill the mansion.

All the cleaning I've done is ruined. There is no order. Every object is out of place. I shout at them, "Get out."

They do not respond. Slowly, as though drugged, I walk around the kitchen, picking up the dented cans from the floor and placing them back into the pantry. I sweep up the crumbs of cereal and throw them into the trash. As soon as I finish a task, the ghosts appear and throw everything back onto the floor. I move into the living room. I am not strong enough to lift the toppled grandfather clock back up. The mirrors lie shattered. I clean and clean, until I hear a terrible sound. Pages being ripped from a book.

I run frantically to the library. My books. All my precious books have been torn apart. The words have been severed from their sentences. It is impossible to make meaning out of them. The language cannot conjure entire worlds inside my head anymore. The characters cannot come to life. They are dead. They can take no action. Their conflicts are forever unresolved.

Pages from different books mix together on the floor. I try to separate them, to organize them into the stories they belong to. But the difficulty of the task overwhelms me.

The children have taken over the mansion. Their memories have taken over my mind. I stand in the library as they run through the halls. I give up right then. I give up ownership of the mansion to the ghosts. I already know what will happen if I fight. I accept the fate given to me.

"Come play with us," they shout.

9

In the opposite direction of the farm lies a dirt path leading to the town. I don't know what I will do there. I am simply walking to get away from the children. The serenity of the walk is a blessing. I breathe in the crisp air. I am delighted that there is not a ghost in sight. I lie down in the grass for a moment and curl myself into the stillness of this clear day. Next to me is a pond, and I watch ducks swim across the surface.

No one has followed me from the mansion. If I don't go back tonight, would Father even notice? Would he go out searching for me? I want him to think I am dead. I want him to be overwhelmed with guilt.

I feel my strength coming back. Energy flows from the ground into my body. Perhaps the world outside is not an illusion. Perhaps it is a source of strength. And the mansion is the real source of my pain.

Father was right. The town is full of excitement. The streets are lined with buildings and vendors and restaurants. The ghosts fill the area, but they pay no attention to me. This is an absolute joy. They don't know what I really am. They assume I am just like them, and they want absolutely nothing from me. I am free to do anything under this veil of anonymity.

The ghosts shop for fruits and vegetables in the market. They pick out cuts of meat. They argue with the sellers to lower the prices. They have full lives here and are absorbed in the small concerns of their routines.

I sit on a bench in a park. No one approaches me. I am left completely alone.

Eventually, I resume my wandering and come across a familiar sight: Father.

He has entered town, and his presence does not go unnoticed. As he walks through the market, pedestrians meet his gaze and wave to him. Vendors shout to get his attention, offering him special discounts on their products. Everyone looks genuinely happy to see him. He stops frequently to talk to ghosts and listen to how their day is going. What has he done to garner so much admiration from them? Was I not born from him? Did he not rescue me and give me a second life? He has an openness, a devotion to seeing goodness in the ghosts that puts them at ease. I cannot summon that kind of devotion inside me. I expect betrayal at every turn.

I follow him to a restaurant. I cannot go inside. Instead I watch him through a window. He sits at a bar, and a ghost pours him a glass of dark liquid. Father drinks and chats with the ghosts sitting beside him. They look like close friends. They slap each other's backs and laugh together. They move to a pool table. Father concentrates on his shot. He doesn't want to lose. But the ghosts are good too. They sink ball after ball. Father challenges them to another game and they play and drink and laugh.

Somehow, I am reassured by this other life of his. Is this the change he meant? To have an ordinary life full of friends and camaraderie? He is important to so many people. He has a special place in their town. They think of him constantly and miss him when he is not around. He knows his life has meaning beyond the small world of the mansion.

The afternoon passes by. I cannot pull myself away from the window. I feel a renewed intimacy with Father that might end at any moment. They finish playing pool. Before they leave, a woman approaches Father. They embrace each other. I sense that he has been waiting for her this whole time. As they converse, the expression on his face changes. It turns grim and pale, but the ghost is not perturbed. She runs her fingers down his jaw, and then she kisses him on the cheek.

I am unable to breathe.

The other ghosts shout and act as if they have witnessed something scandalous. Father and the woman continue to touch each other's arms and faces.

I pull away from the window. I am filled with revulsion. I question everything Father has been doing. What role has this woman played in his decisions?

I have rarely thought of Mother. There has not been a need to. Father, for the most part, has taken care of my every need. If I felt an emptiness, I assumed it came from my lack of knowledge about the ghosts, how I would never truly understand my role in this world or why I am so different from them.

The characters in my books led me to believe that I had a mother in my previous life who could not follow me into this world. I cannot remember her, but sometimes, as I read, I find small details that flower vividly within me. Long, flowing black hair. Shimmering brown eyes. Gentle hands.

Perhaps if Mother were around, Father would not have changed so drastically. He would not have wanted a life beyond the mansion. I wonder if she would take my side in this dilemma. If she would have protected me from the children. There is no way to know. I did not grow up with Mother in this world. And now it is much too late for her to appear again in my life.

I walk around the town and push the questions that I have about the woman at the bar from my mind. I try to walk quickly enough for new sights and sounds to distract me, but panic rises as a physical pain. There is a mounting pressure in my stomach. A stiffness holding my limbs. Ghosts continue to walk past me. They do not notice me at all. My anonymity, earlier a comfort, becomes another source of pain. I have no one I can go to, no one whom I can share my thoughts with. Returning to the mansion is not an option. The children are most likely still there. I long for the safe enclosure of the attic. The window that lets me see everything from above.

Evening descends over the town. The sun sets. Shadows spill from the sky. They crawl across the ground, and wrap themselves around the buildings. Their darkness is opaque. Once they cover the buildings, all the physical features disappear, as though the buildings are trapped in black sheets of metal. Around me, dark shapes replace the town.

I enter a church that is still identifiable. I have always loved churches in books. This one is quiet. The pews are empty. I love the idea of sitting in the back, listening to a wise man deliver a sermon full of wisdom and hope. Does someone like that exist in this world? Is it possible for entities other than ghosts to reside in the afterlife?

There is one other presence in the church. The ghost Father has been fixated on. He smiles and nods at me. Then he directs his gaze forward at the candlelit altar and the crucifix above it. I stare at him. A fury rises up in me. My face is hot. My hands shake. He is calm and collected as always. I want to do something to unravel him. He is the only ghost at the farm that acts without a discernible motive.

"You do not deserve to exist," I say. "You and your people do not deserve Father's help."

He does not turn to face me.

"Are you listening? Do you know what those children did today? They destroyed my home. They broke everything inside of it. No one stopped them. Why do you let them do that?" My voice fills the dim church.

"I have no control over them," the ghost says. "I do not approve of what they're doing, but I have no control. I'm sorry for what they did to you. I know you must have been in pain."

"How do you know? You don't care if I'm in pain or not. You're just saying meaningless words."

"I mean every word I say."

"No, you don't."

"I know that you are a kind boy, that you deserve to be loved, and that those children were wrong to hurt you."

"Stop talking," I say. "Stop saying words like that. You don't mean them."

"I want things to change," the ghost says. "I watch us every day, and I wish we could change. It pains me deeply that we can't. That we exist in denial of our fate when we must accept what we really are. We must accept the darkness ahead."

"I don't believe you. I bet you're helping those children. They want to see me suffer because I have what they want. I have what they can never have."

"Death changes us," he says. "But we do not always change for the better."

"Why does Father love you?" I ask. "What have you done for him?"

"He treats me like he treats everyone else. He wants love too."

"He cares more about what you think. You're different from the rest."

"I do not want what the others do. I fear my own existence. I fear the harm that I am capable of. I want your father to stop helping us."

"You have power over him," I say. "You are wrong about change being impossible. Father is changing constantly. I no longer recognize him. He doesn't love me anymore. I want him to love me again."

"He still loves you. He loves you more than anyone else in the world. But he is tormented. He had a whole life before you arrived here. And he is helpless for the first time in a while."

"Stop it," I say. "Stop telling me lies."

"You have assumed too much about us," he says. "We are more than what you see."

Father's friend is no different from the children. All of the ghosts exist to drive you mad. They manipulate you with nonsense. I want to hurt him. I want to erase his existence. Then maybe Father will come back. I start to sob. The tears pour out uncontrollably. I try to hide my face. Father's friend grabs my arms. He has finally had enough. He wants to harm me. He is going to devour my soul.

"You poor child," he says and holds me against his chest. He rubs my shoulder. "Someday you won't be so afraid. Someday you'll realize you have nothing to fear."

• • •

The doors to the church open. Father's friend pulls me to the corner and shuts me inside a confessional booth. The church fills with footsteps. I hear Father's voice and a woman addressing him. I push the door of the booth slightly open and, through the crack, I see the area where they've gathered. I'm far enough away for them not to notice me. A coffin has been placed beneath the crucifix. The woman whispers something to Father, and he nods. He lifts the lid, and steps into the coffin. He lies down and closes his eyes. The ghosts gather around him, their voices melding into a cacophony of whispers. That's when the thought occurs to me: this is his work. This is his role among the ghosts that he has been trying to escape.

Every morning he left the mansion to give his body over to the ghosts. One at a time, they possessed him. They marveled at how it felt to have flesh again, to experience the sensations of touch, to see the fields vividly, to hear the enchantment of birdsong, and to taste the wonders of food. What torture, I think. To die for half the day, his consciousness suppressed and torn to shreds, just so the ghosts can have a mortal body again. But he has lost the ability. The ghosts cannot possess him anymore. They cannot possess me either. I won't let them and they will go mad with longing.

Someone shoves the door to the confessional booth shut. I throw my weight against it. I pound my fists. But it won't open. Surely Father will hear me. Surely the ghosts will. And they will drag me out and I will tell them that they've taken advantage of Father for long enough. He will never lie in the coffin for them again.

The whispering stops. The shuffle of footsteps dies down, and the church is completely quiet. I press lightly on the door, and it opens without resistance. I step into the nave, and the emptiness alarms me. All the ghosts are gone. Only the coffin, now closed, remains. When I open it, Father is not inside. I touch the white cloth lining. His warmth lingers on my fingertips. Where could he have possibly gone? I crawl inside and lie down, facing the ceiling. I imagine everything inside me going dark. The lid slams shut. I can't get out.

I float in the darkness for a long time, dreaming of Father, wishing we hadn't been born here, but in the land of the living. I move my hands and notice something strange. The membrane of cloth is gone. Instead, I feel the softness of soil. I push my arms up and there is no resistance from the lid of the coffin. I am able to sit up freely. I stare into the abyss.

"Hello? Can someone hear me?"

I dig my fingers through the soil and squeeze to remind myself that I am alive, and will return to the visible world again. The sounds of footsteps emerge in the distance, and I hear a door squeak open. High above, a ray of light shines down, revealing the concrete walls that surround me. A dark figure stands in front of the light and speaks. "Are you down here?" The figure waits.

I notice a set of stairs leading to the floor. "Come on. Don't be like this."

I am too afraid to respond.

"I'll be in the hospital only for a few weeks. I'll be out before you know it."

I squeeze the soil. The voice is so familiar.

"Don't you want to say good-bye before I leave?"

I squint at the dark figure. I go through my memories.

"Please, talk to me."

"I'm here."

"Honey, did you find him?"

"Yes," the dark figure shouts. "He's hiding in the basement."

"Well, tell him to come out. We have to leave soon."

I stand up and run to the stairs as quickly as I can. I approach the dark figure, hoping to see who this woman is. I enter the light. And everything disappears. The darkness is stripped away. The ceiling of the church shines overhead, and I am lying in the coffin again. The lid has been lifted and Father's friend gazes down at me. He drags me out of the coffin, and says, "You shouldn't be in there."

"Where was I?" I ask.

Father's friend turns grim. "You shouldn't have seen that. You need to go home."

"Seen what?" I say.

"Go," he shouts and pushes me out of the church doors.

10

When I return to the mansion, it is completely clean. The floor has been swept and mopped. The pantry and cupboards are fully stocked with food. The furniture in each room has been put back in its rightful place. Even the library has returned to its former state, with all of the books organized on the shelves, each one's pages intact. There are not even traces of tears.

"Hello?" I shout, expecting the children to be hiding somewhere. But the air is still and I know they are truly gone.

When Father comes home, he tells me how cheerful and radiant I look. He asks what I did today. I am too scared to know the truth, to learn who Father really is. And so, I tell him about the wonderful time I had playing with the ghosts. And he is happy. He has no reason not to be.

Father gestures for me to sit with him on the sofa. He apologizes for his absence these past days, but he was working on a plan. He announces that he has found someone to take over his role among the ghosts.

Father met Madame on the night he went into town to retrieve my medicine. She was a customer at the pharmacy. He arrived there in a panic, out of breath, barely able to speak. She was calm and patient. She listened to him carefully and then relayed his message to the pharmacist.

Father was deeply impressed by her poise and self-assurance. Any worries he had disappeared in her presence. He quickly began to crave the person he was whenever she was nearby. He was going to tell me much sooner, but he feared how I would react. So much was changing in our lives. He wanted to wait until I had adjusted, until I had stepped out into the world.

I am overcome with despair at the knowledge that I was the one to unite them. How cruel fate is for my plan to lead to such outcomes. I wish he'd never told me about Madame and kept his affair a secret for eternity. I resent his honesty. It brought nothing but pain.

I tell Father how happy I am for him. How marvelous it is that he has found someone to love. He embraces me, and decides to plan a gathering for the three of us.

"This is the solution," Father says. "Madame has the ability to grant the ghosts what they want."

I nod. I excuse myself. In my room, I try to sleep. I try to stop thinking of the changes in the world around me. When I am unable to rest, I bring a hammer back to my room. I smash all the medicine. I savor the excruciating sound of the impact as the pills crumble. I bundle the fine powder in a cloth and creep to the kitchen. I pour it into the leftover shepherd's pie that Father loves so much.

．．．

Our routine changes on the day I am supposed to meet Madame. Father does not leave to work on the farm. He hums and sings as he showers and gets dressed. I stay in bed for as long as possible. When he pokes his head into my room, I say I am more tired than usual and need more time to sleep.

"We're going to be late," he shouts. "We don't want to be late. Let's make a good impression today, all right?" I pull the blanket off and take a deep breath. I say I am excited to meet her.

As we approach the door, Father stops me and says, "This is the day. I can feel it. This is the day I've been telling you about. Everything will change."

We make our way through the farmland, and I am startled by how quiet it is. No laughter, no conversation. The ghosts are gone. They are not in the wheat fields. They are not feeding their livestock. Even the children are absent from the playground.

"Why is it so quiet? Where did they all go?"

"They're not working today," Father says. "They have other things they need to take care of."

My unease is worse now that I don't know their whereabouts. We pass their houses, and all the doors and windows are open. Plates of half-eaten food lie on their tables. Chairs have been knocked over.

"Where does Madame live?" I ask.

"Deep in the forest," he says.

"But you said you met her in the town."

"We're not meeting her in the town today."

Father is smiling, but now there is a darkness in his eyes. He keeps looking over his shoulder, as though something is following us. He tells me to walk faster, and I hear the raggedness of his breath. I want to know what he is seeing behind us, but there is only the farm, there is only the mansion and the shadow it casts.

The forest is dense with foliage. Father has to push branches out of the way to make a path for me. I hate how they scrape against my arms and legs, leaving red scratches. The air is stifling. Dew covers the leaves. As we walk, I can barely see the sky through the canopy, and eventually the path back to the mansion has completely disappeared. Father guides us with remarkable assurance. He doesn't hesitate before any step he takes.

"How do you know where you're going?" I ask.

"It's a clear path," he says. "Keep up. I don't want you to fall behind."

"You have to slow down."

"If we don't go faster, we'll be late. We shouldn't make her worry."

"I'm trying my best. I'm going as fast as I can."

The foliage grows denser. Vines hang off the branches and snag my shoulders, as though they are purposely dragging me back. The bushes barely budge as I weave around them. My shoes sink into the mud.

I look up, and Father is noticeably farther away. His large back has shrunk with distance. He fades right into the trees.

"Slow down!" I scream as Father disappears.

No path presents itself to me. Every direction appears exactly the same. I am overwhelmed by uncertainty. I do not know if I will find my way to Father, or if I will travel farther away from him and be lost within the forest. My legs refuse to move.

Surely, he will realize what has happened and come back to find me. He will find me if I stay still.

Then the vines slither up my arms and around my torso. The leaves thicken in size. The forest holds me in place.

I imagine the orderly mansion, each room with its prescribed function. I imagine I am still there, lying on the sofa, eating a nice meal, or taking a warm bath. Yes, Father will appear at any moment. He is here. He is by my side.

"How much longer are you going to wait?" a voice asks.

I look around, but there is no one. He has hidden himself among the trees.

"Show yourself!" I scream.

"You can see me. I am right in front of you."

There is nothing to protect me here. The vines tighten their grip around my body.

"I've been following you since you entered the forest. I knew you would get lost."

"Who are you?"

"I go by many names. What do you want to call me?"

I shake my head. He's trying to distract me. "You must know where Father is. Can you please tell him where I am?"

"I can. But he won't listen. He is too busy heading to his destination. Nothing can make him turn back."

"He'll turn back for me. He cares about me more than anything in the world."

"But you're alone. He left you behind."

"He didn't realize what happened. It's my fault for not keeping up."

"You're just a child. It's not your fault. He should have slowed down. He should have thought more about you."

"Can you point the way? Just point the way, and I'll leave your forest. I won't be a bother to you much longer."

"You're that child in the mansion. We all know about you."

"This is my first time in the forest. I just need a little help."

"Everyone knows their way through the forest. We all have to live here at one point. We're not all so lucky as to be born in that beautiful mansion."

"It's not my home anymore," I say.

"Oh? Then where is your home?"

"Wherever Father is."

The voice laughs so loudly that it seems to come from the sky itself. "How devoted you are. How touching. I can help you, but only if you give up the hope that your father will come back. I want you to accept that you have lost him."

"No. I don't need your help. You're not even here. You can't do anything."

The voice continues to laugh. The leaves tremble. They fall and cover me all the way up to my waist.

"You should accept help when it is offered. What I'm asking you to do is not difficult. It is merely facing reality. How much longer can you wait?"

I struggle against the vines. They are too strong. I feel my body grow weaker. I can barely think. I want to fall asleep, but I fear what might happen to me if I do. I watch sunlight fade through the canopy. Darkness drenches the air. Hunger seizes me. My stomach moans. My mouth is dry. I dream of water, the taste of Father's cooking. I'll say anything, agree to anything, no matter the consequences.

But the voice has been silent for a long time. He doesn't answer when I call out to him. Again and again, I find myself abandoned. Something terrible is asked of me and I can't bring myself to do it. Why are the conditions of love, of rescue, so difficult to achieve? Why do they rarely align with what I am capable of? I don't know what to sacrifice. All my desires appear equally important. I have no clarity about what truly matters. I cannot determine what will give my existence meaning in this world.

Then I hear a noise coming from far away. I think it is the source of the voice returning to antagonize me, before I realize the sound is someone panting. It is Father. He is gasping for air running away from something. The noise surrounds me, echoing from different directions.

It is not me who needs rescue, but Father. He is being chased. Metal chains rattle. He is frantic and afraid, and he needs me to find him. The vines strain against my skin. I jerk my arms and my legs against them, but it is no use. Something powerful is keeping me back.

"Leave me alone!" Father shouts. His voice is so loud I feel like he is right in front of me even though I know he is far away.

Leaves rustle. The sounds of footsteps crash over my ears. A stampede of them chasing after Father.

I continue to struggle against the vines. I claw and kick as they hold me down. I struggle until the noises are gone and the darkness of the forest writhes silently with the inexplicable.

Rescue eventually comes. It comes, but I do not know if my rescuers are friends or enemies. There are footsteps through the darkness, this time much gentler. A line of ghosts in black robes moves past me holding lanterns. They pass as though I do not exist to them. The light from their lanterns does not reveal the branches or vines around us, only more darkness.

I move my arms and am met with no restraint. I am able to move freely now, but there is nowhere to go, no one to run after. Freedom without direction is a trap. I watch the line of ghosts. They are humming and chanting. Their voices remind me of the ghosts from the farm. I cannot see their faces. I am terribly cold. The ghosts at the end of the line are carrying a coffin. I see in the dim light that the coffin is small and beautiful, with ornate carvings on the wood. I walk to the end of the line and follow the ghosts.

"Hold this," a ghost says.

"We need your help."

I grip the bottom of the coffin. It is immensely heavy. The longer we walk, the heavier it feels. Eventually we arrive at a clearing where a hole has already been dug, a tombstone standing at its edge. Grass and flowers sway around the grave, but beyond them are only shadows.

I let go of the coffin as the ghosts lower it into the hole. All around me, sobs erupt from the mouths of the ghosts. They throw their heads back in grief. Several of them fall onto their knees and pound the ground with their fists. They are breaking apart.

I did not know they were capable of expressing sorrow like this. Their reactions are overwhelming, and yet I am startled by how genuine they appear. They all seem to possess profound love for the ghost in the coffin.

. . .

"We have gathered here today to mourn the passing of one of our own," a ghost says. She stands at the edge of the grave and raises her hands. "This child lived a joyful life with us, and now it is time for him to move on. He has made peace with his past, and no longer needs the blessing of our company. It is unfortunate that so many of our little ones pass away so quickly. Their hearts hold less pain, and they do not need as much help as the other members of our community. As such, they're a source of great wonder for us. Such wonder, of course, cannot last very long. If it does, then it becomes ordinary. We must accept that their existence is meant to be brief. Rise, you must all rise. This child would not want you to behave in such an uncontrolled manner. Rise and offer your tribute."

He's dead. The child who terrorized me and destroyed my home is dead. The rest of the children will join him. I will outlive them. This is what I wanted, for them to pay, to suffer a cruel fate. I smile. The harder the ghosts cry, the happier I become. I know the truth. He has not moved on to another world. He has simply stopped existing. He is now in a place where he cannot laugh his ridiculous laugh, where he cannot play his terrible games. The ghosts mourn for nothing. They mourn for beings that do not deserve such sympathy.

"It's your turn," a ghost says, shoving me toward the grave. "Mourn for him. Offer your tribute."

"I have nothing to give him."

"It is tradition. Everyone must mourn."

"I feel nothing for him. I'm happy he's gone."

"This is not a choice. You will pay your respects."

"He deserves his fate. His life brought me nothing but terror."

"He was only doing what you needed him to."

I laugh. I spit on his coffin. I hurl handfuls of soil. "You all hated him too. Don't lie. You all wanted him gone too. His life was worthless."

The ghosts force me onto my knees. They shove my head into the grave. The air smells like vomit and excrement. "Grieve for him. Say you owe your life to him."

I burst into sobs. "No, I want Father," I say. "Where is he? Take me to him. Take me to him."

The ghosts throw me into the grave. I crash into the coffin. I do not open it. I know there is nothing inside. The child has disappeared. Once he ceases to exist, nothing gets left behind. His body, which was never real, evaporates. This funeral is for nothing. This grave holds emptiness. They mourn the emptiness. They worship it.

The light from the lanterns begins to fade from the edge of the grave. The light is my way out of the writhing darkness of the forest. I know this is my only chance. I stand on the coffin. The wood starts to splinter beneath my feet. Before it cracks, I launch myself at the edge of the grave, but my hands slip, and I fall back down. The light continues to recede.

I turn around to stand on what is left of the coffin and try again, but it has opened, and I cannot believe what I'm seeing.

I face the person inside: Father.

I touch Father's face. I squint. His eyes are closed. His skin is cold. He is still breathing. I feel his pulse, then listen to the steady beat of his heart.

"Wake up," I say, shaking him. "Why are you here? What happened to you?" I shake him, but he stays asleep. He's not dead. I know this. He can't be. He'll wake up any minute now. I try not to think about the ceremony. How happy I was. How I refused to mourn the person in the grave. But it was supposed to be the child. The child. Not Father, who looks so small and innocent crammed into the coffin. His limbs are squeezed tightly against his torso for him to fit.

"Father, wake up," I say. "I'm sorry I didn't mourn for you. I'm sorry I couldn't change. Will you wake up if I do?"

Father's heartbeat grows louder and louder until it feels like we are inside of his rib cage. And we are safe. Nothing can take us. I hold my fists high up in the air and slam them down on his chest. Father gasps awake.

11

Moonlight breaks through the canopy. The darkness scatters like moths, and the trees of the forest sway above us, their branches soaking up the light. Father takes a moment to regain his strength before he lifts me over the edge of the grave. He winces. I climb onto the ground, and then I help pull him up. How much time has already passed? I've never spent an entire night away from the mansion before. The forest rustles with soft sounds. Father looks around us as though to make sure we're truly alone. He moves to different areas and pushes back the branches. He peers forward in search of a way out.

We rest near a small patch of flowers. Father holds out his palms, and sitting on them are clusters of berries. "You must be hungry," he says. "Go on, have some. I made sure they're safe to eat."

"What about you? Are you going to have some?"

"I ate a few already. I'm not hungry."

I eat the berries slowly, and when I am done, I tell him, "I thought you were dead. I thought I lost you for good."

Father leans away from the moonlight. I can't read his expression.

"The ghosts were chasing you. They turned against you. It was all pretend, the kindness they were showing us. They were just waiting for the right time to attack."

"That wasn't the ghosts," Father says.

"Then who were they?"

"Will you believe me if I tell you?"

I whisper that I will.

"There is a greater threat in this world," Father says. "That threat is our memories. They're not just something inside our minds. They're as real as any object—these trees, the berries, the farm, the mansion. All the memories of our lives in the world of living move like water in an underground river hidden in this forest. The ghosts are full of longing to see those memories again, but have no access to them. My role is to help them visit their memories. It's what I've done for so long. Every morning, I left the mansion and went to the forest and I brought a ghost onto a boat. There we sat together, and when I closed my eyes, I could see it, the memory that they so desperately wished to relive, and then that memory rose from the river, and wrapped itself around us, around the boat, and the ghost entered the world of that memory. They could see a loved one again, kiss them and hold them. They could hear laughter and feel the joy of that day or night. It was a process that brought the ghosts much peace, and allowed them to move on. Since we are human, we have greater access to our senses and emotions. But this sensitivity also means that the work can be perilous. It is easy for the emotions of one memory to conjure the emotions of another. And the river holds all memories, even the darkest ones. It took all of my strength to keep the dark memories away, to shelter the ghosts in their happier ones. Sometimes I wasn't careful enough, and the ghosts saw something they shouldn't have, and they lost control, burdened with grief. It was very difficult, very painful, to stay calm and compassionate in order to guide them back to safety. I didn't want that kind of life for you. I didn't want you to be consumed with the ghosts' darkest memories. Their past lives are not yours."

"No, that can't be," I say. "That's not your role. You exist for the ghosts to possess you, so they can know what it's like to have a body again. They hurt you so they can be alive."

"You told me you were ready," Father said.

"I am."

"The ghosts do not possess us. It is the living who possess the ghosts."

"That's not possible. They're evil. They'll do anything to convince you to trust them. You've been possessed by them for too long."

"Enough, no more of these childish arguments. Listen to me, we are in danger, but you have to see the real threat. I've lost my ability. I can't help the ghosts retrieve their memories anymore. I've tried many times, but we see nothing. Only the silence of the river speaks back to us. At first, I thought it would be fine if I stopped my work for a while. I thought I could help the ghosts create a life around the mansion. The farms, and their houses, and the activities in the town. But their longing for a taste of the past is much too strong. And their longing fed the darkness within the memories, and the memories went mad. They left the river in search of the ghosts who belonged to them. Have you seen the shadows?" Father asks. "The thick, opaque shadows stretched over the land? Blanketing the buildings? Those are the memories, searching for their hosts. Soon enough, all the memories will leave the river and cover the sky and land in total darkness, replacing the things we hold so dear. It will be an eternal night, and we won't be able to see or taste or touch the material pleasures of this world anymore. They will belong to the past, the unreachable land of the living. The darkness will terrorize the ghosts with unspeakable longing."

I think about the dark shapes I witnessed. I tremble. "Yes," I say. "I've seen the shadows. I've been inside them."

"I thought you could replace me," Father says. "I thought you could satisfy their longing. But how can I place such a burden on you? How can I ask you to put yourself through such a trial? You should still have a life of your own. You should be free. It is my responsibility to find another solution."

The moonlight wanes. Father's face becomes more difficult to read.

"I can do it. I can try," I say. "I want to be useful."

"The responsibility will tear you apart. You are not ready."

"But we will lose everything. Everyone will suffer a fate worse than death. That's what you predicted."

"It is not a task that can be done so easily. You cannot perform the union of ghost and memory out of fear and desperation, or because you want to please me. You must truly understand the ghosts, you must care for them the way you do for me. Have you reached that point?"

I lower my head.

"If we try," Father continues, "and things end poorly, I will lose you too. I will lose you to the river of memories, and then all will truly be lost."

"Don't say that," I say. "I will be ready. I will be strong enough."

And Father leans into the moonlight, and smiles as though he believes me.

12

In the distance, there is a light. A light shining from the mansion. And we follow it like a star to find our way out of the forest. The sun grips the horizon, and peeks its head over, slowly pulling itself up as we walk through the grass. We pass the farmland with its rows of crops. But that's not all that is there. Long, opaque shadows stretch across the field like tears in the fabric of the landscape. I stand on the edge of a shadow and touch its surface. The shadow writhes. It is as cold as metal.

"It's asleep," Father says.

"Can you see into it? Do you know whose memory this is?"

"No," he says. "It is all darkness to me. I'm no different from the ghosts."

We keep walking, and there are more impenetrable shadows, standing in various shapes. They cover the homes of the ghosts. They cover patches of the farmland. The shadows contrast greatly with the details and colors of the material world. They don't react to the wind or the light. They offer nothing to the senses but coldness. I know why it is so quiet. The ghosts have run away. They are hiding.

We reach the mansion. As soon as I open the door, I know something is wrong.

Everything looks the same. All the rooms are arranged in the same configurations. All the furniture is in the right place. But the air is stiff and tense. It smells like the dirt around Father's grave. The mirrors reflect a dim version of the room. Is this the same mansion I grew up in? Or am I still in the forest? Perhaps I have not escaped, and the shadows led me deeper into their home.

"What are you doing here? Who let you inside?" a ghost shouts. He is standing at the top of the stairs. He is wearing a suit and a gold monocle.

"This used to be my home," I say. "I lived here. Who are you?"

"How dare you lie like that. This is Madame's estate. She wouldn't appreciate you making such claims. Leave!"

"You're the intruder! I'm not going anywhere."

The ghost stomps down the stairs. "Can you prove it? What proof do you have of ownership? Madame has all the paperwork in her safe. What do you have?"

"I don't need papers. I know what's mine. This has to be my home."

"You're lucky I'm not a violent man. I wouldn't lay a finger on you. It would be utterly beneath me."

"I'm the son of the man who built this mansion. He'll sort this out. He's all the proof I need."

But when I turn around to seek Father's assistance, he isn't there.

No one is at the door. Outside, the shadows in the field squirm, and I try not to think about the worst possibility.

He must be somewhere in the mansion. He must be. The ghost slips past me and slams the door closed.

"What are you looking at? Madame is the true owner. No one ever comes to this mansion. They all know their place."

"Where did you take him?" I ask the ghost.

"Who?"

"Father."

The ghost laughs. "I've had enough of your squabbling."

I run past the ghost and find my way up the stairs.

"Stop!" he yells. "Stop!"

I hear him panting behind me.

I dart inside the library. I lock the door and place all my weight against it. The ghost says I can't stay in there forever, that he's going to bring the guards to drag me out of Madame's mansion. Then I hear him walk away, and I can finally let myself relax for a moment. I have no clue what is happening to me. All I know is that I can't leave this mansion, no matter who it belongs to. Nothing good can come from entering the outside world again.

I recognize all the books in the library. They are in the exact order that I placed them. I flip through the pages of *The Voyage of the Dawn Treader*, then *The Complete Grimm's Fairy Tales*, and *Metamorphoses*, hoping to find some sort of clue in the words. They are all blank. They have no words on them. Their stories are gone.

I don't remember if Father ever showed me any paperwork for the mansion. It never even occurred to me that we needed proof of ownership. I am terribly aware of my predicament. This Madame who Father wanted me to meet has plenty of ghosts protecting her, while I have no one. I unlock the door and peek out into the hall. It is empty.

The ghost from earlier is on the first floor, yelling. His voice echoes throughout the mansion. I walk quietly down the steps and catch a glimpse of a group of ghosts. They look terrified.

"We have an intruder in our midst!" he says. "How did he get in? Who let him in? You all are supposed to be guarding the door. Does Madame's safety mean nothing to you? If she gets hurt because of your negligence, there will be hell to pay. You will never be able to find work again. I don't care if you have to break down the door. Capture the insolent child as soon as possible."

I spot someone familiar in the group: the ghost Father has been fixated on. He must work for this Madame now. I know he'll help me.

The mansion might belong to someone else, but I have a better sense of its layout than the ghosts. Whenever they are near, I am able to find a different route or hiding spot to continue to evade them. I am small and can fit into corners that they don't even think to check. I make my way toward the kitchen. The path is treacherous, but in the living room I hide inside of the grandfather clock.

I am certain I will find my way to Father's friend. There is a reason he has appeared again and again in my life whenever Father is not around. I hear his voice from the kitchen and head in that direction.

I hide behind the entrance until the kitchen is quiet. I peek around the wall, and Father's friend is alone at the counter. The other ghosts have left through the back exit. I run madly toward him and pull him through the basement door. We stand at the top of the dark stairs, Father's friend still holding the knife he was using to cut the meat. The light from the kitchen illuminates the panels of the door, framing us. He does not look surprised to see me. His face is expressionless, as always.

"I have to finish preparing the meal," he says.

"Don't you remember me?" I ask.

"I do. But I am not finished with the meal yet, and it is almost Madame's dinner time."

"Who cares about her meal?" I say. "You have to help me."

"What can I possibly help you with?"

And when I try to think of an answer, my mind goes blank.

"You can leave the mansion right now. No one is stopping you. You can return to your home."

"But this is my home," I say. "It has to be."

"It's an easy mistake to make," he says. "There are duplicates in this world. You would know if you'd explored it more. Your mansion is one of many of the same model. You're lost. You must find your way back."

"That's what I need you to help me with."

"I have my work to do. I cannot give it all up to help you. What will you offer me? Madame treats me well and guarantees my safety. I am not afraid when I am here."

"I'm not like everyone else in this world," I say. "I'm a human being. I deserve your help."

"You don't deserve to be safe just because you are human. I will not risk my safety for you."

"But you're connected to Father. You're loyal to him, and I'm his son."

"Do you mean the man who has abandoned you? That's who I should be loyal to? I want absolutely nothing to do with him. He's a weak, tormented man."

"What?" I say. "He didn't abandon anyone. They did something to him, the ghosts and their shadows. He's in danger."

"Is that what you think? If I take you to where you need to go, will you finally leave me be?"

"Yes, take me."

From the bottom of the stairs, sounds travel up to us. Metal chains. Groaning. "What's down there?" I ask.

"Follow me," Father's friend says, and he guides me away from the basement, up to the second floor. We run into no other ghosts. I hear no sounds of them cleaning or performing their other duties.

"Is Father in one of these rooms?" I ask.

"I'm taking you to where you need to go," he says.

We reach the entrance to the attic. He knocks, pauses, and then opens the door. Madame sits in front of the window that overlooks the fields and rolling hills.

13

"Madame," Father's friend says, "I've delivered him as you asked."

I stare at him, astonished.

She stands up and faces us. Her long white dress sways over the floor. She is the woman from town who kissed Father on the cheek. My throat tightens.

"Thank you for your services. I hope there wasn't any trouble."

"Of course not. It was my pleasure."

She nods, and he leaves the attic.

I am startled by how beautiful she is, how kind she appears, how faint I feel in her presence. I almost forget the betrayal from Father's friend.

"You must be very confused," she says. "I'm sorry for everything you've been through. I wish I could have made things easier. Would you like something to drink? Any food?"

I place a hand on my stomach. I am struck by how hungry I am. The last time I ate was the evening when Father and I were still together.

Madame gestures to a tray of sandwiches and milk. I greedily eat them, thinking only of my next bite.

Behind me, Madame laughs. "There's plenty more. Eat as much as you like. You were in the forest for so long. You must be starving."

I stop eating right then. The food doesn't settle well in my stomach.

"The ghosts told me you were separated from your father in the forest. He must have been very worried. Things like that can happen there. He should have been more careful. At least now you're safe."

Her voice is having an odd effect on me. She gives me the same sensation that Father gave me back before he changed.

"I know you've gone through a lot. But there's no reason to be afraid of me. I'm the person your father wants you to meet."

"Where is he? Why can't I find him?"

"He's resting. Today has been hard on him. He's made a tough decision. Why don't you rest too?"

"I want to see him."

"Now is not the time to disturb him. We need to let him sleep first. I know you're scared, but you're completely safe with me. No one can hurt you or your father here. Sit next to me. Let's share the view. Your father told me how much you love looking through the window. It's beautiful out there."

I sit down. A voice inside of me tells me to leave. That this woman is more dangerous than she lets on. But she is right. I am tired. I am tired of running, of being afraid.

Even if I leave, I have nowhere to go. Father won't be waiting for me at home.

Outside, on the rolling hills, the remaining houses of the ghosts light up with candles and lamps. Inside a few of them, families sit near their kitchen window and eat a meal. Below the hills, deer gather around a black pond. It is astonishing to me how similar everything is to our region. The arrangement of the farmland, the stables for the livestock, the forest on the horizon. If I let myself, I can believe I am at home. I can pretend the shadows are just a part of the night

True to her word, Madame takes good care of me. I am well fed and warmly clothed. Plates of food appear on the kitchen counter, still hot as though the ghosts quickly left. I receive plenty of rest and quiet for two days. When I walk around the mansion, no one is there to disturb me. Even Madame has disappeared from the attic.

The ghosts on the outside do not come near the front door. They do not knock on it and demand me to let them inside. The only unwelcome noise drifts up from the basement. A subdued groaning and clanking of chains. The door to the basement is locked. I pretend the noise isn't there. It cannot disrupt this dream I'm in.

Eventually, Madame calls my name, and I walk downstairs to see her sitting on the sofa. The ghost who interrogated me when I first arrived is beside her. He stands, and his mouth twists itself into a smile.

"My lord," he shouts. "How glad I am to see you again. You look very well rested today! I hope you've found your stay pleasing."

Madame remains seated. She sips from her cup of tea.

His greeting does not sit well with me. I can't bring myself to respond. I think of his question about my proof of ownership. What belongs to me? How can I know?

The ghost laughs nervously. He glances at Madame and looks momentarily dismayed before he dons his mask of enthusiasm again. "Please," he says. "You have to forgive my past behavior. I did not know who you were. I sincerely apologize for the foolish way I treated you. I've been in agony for the past few days knowing how deeply I wronged you. Of course this place is your home. And I am the one who is the intruder."

My body continues to stiffen. I am unable to address him. I wish he would stop talking and go away. I will not say anything to make him look better in the eyes of Madame, who he constantly glances at as he gives his apology.

"I think that's enough," Madame says. "He's heard you."

The ghost continues to make his case until she smiles at him. He stops immediately, bows, and walks to the kitchen. I brighten at the sight of defeat on his face. I savor this surge of power.

"I'm sorry, again, for his behavior. You have to excuse him. He's been in my employment for centuries, and he's lived in the mansion the entire time. He refuses to go out. He's very fond of this place, and so he's overly protective of it."

"He's never left?" I ask, grimacing at this information.

"No, he doesn't see any point. He has everything he needs in here, and he doesn't interact well with the ghosts outside. He enjoys giving orders too much."

"Well, he shouldn't isolate himself like that," I say. "Maybe then he won't be so rude to others, and he'll treat them better."

Madame laughs. "Yes, he can certainly learn a thing or two from you. He can be very jealous, lashing out at anyone who has my attention. I find it all rather amusing."

I nod, but a part of me squirms at her statement.

"Who do you think you are?" the ghost shouts from the kitchen. "This pie is overcooked. It isn't fit for someone like Madame to eat. You should be ashamed of yourself. Bake it again, and it better be up to my standards!"

My face reddens. I wish he would stop. I wish he wouldn't treat the other ghosts that way. I thank Madame for sorting out the issue, and then I run up the stairs to hide in the library.

I enjoy the serenity with an apprehension that I keep secret from Madame. It is clear how much power she wields over this region of the world, and I sense that it would be unwise to upset her, especially when she holds herself with such poise and care.

Of course, things cannot go on blissfully like this forever. Madame has a plan. She will eventually ask something of me. But this uneasiness is not any worse than the kind I felt in the real mansion with Father, where there was always the pressure to accept the ghosts. This is why I no longer have a strong desire to return to the real mansion. I am forgetting what made our mansion feel safe. I am forgetting what makes me feel like I belong to a place.

Outside, the shadows remain in place. New ones have not yet crept up to terrorize us. The ghosts return to their regular life and work on the farm. They maneuver around the shadows like they are trees. They do not show any signs of the fear that Father mentioned. Is it because of Madame? Does she have the same ability to unite the ghosts with their memories? Is that why she wields so much authority in this region of our world?

Eventually, my curiosity gets the best of me. I want to know more about Madame, especially if she is the person who Father loves and who knows where he has gone.

We are in the attic again, watching the ghosts work in the fields. One strange difference between the ones here and the ones in my region is that these ghosts do not feign happiness. They are somber, as though they are too weary to deny the fate ahead of them.

I ask Madame what Father has told her about me.

"He has expressed deep love for you. It is the kind of love that has made him very afraid."

I narrow my eyes. "It doesn't seem like he loves me anymore. He's so caught up in the problems of this world.

Something is always going wrong, and he keeps forcing me to do things I can't."

"That's what love does," Madame says. "You can see only the fears right in front of you. You can act only in response to those fears. Try to prevent them from happening. He is afraid you will go down the wrong path in life. But his perceptions are based on his own experiences, which differ from yours. This is the source of much of his agony. What he thought was right turned out to be wrong. And he cannot find a way to keep this world safe for you. To show you his love without hurting you. There is difficulty in forming such attachments. If he indulges your desires, then there is a chance you will not be able to withstand the suffering that all life must endure. That is your wish, correct? To stay inside the mansion for eternity?"

"Yes."

"Your father understands that. He knows exactly what you want. But desire often prevents us from growing. You cannot stay a child forever. You must face uncertainty. That is the purpose of existence: for the heart to bend. You will see much beauty once you've confronted what you thought was impossible to endure. But you have not responded well to our world, have you? He has not shown his sorrow to you, but in private he has wept at the sight of you in pain. He has questioned himself. He doesn't know what is true. Is pain necessary to your growth? Is there no path in which pain can be avoided? These questions have greatly unraveled him."

As I listen to Madame, a weariness washes through me. Her words are not making any sense. It seems that Father has made something complicated out of something very simple. Yes, he is lost. That much I understand. But why would love drag him away from me? Why would he ever leave the person he loves? He should follow them. He should follow them and never turn back.

"You doubt me, don't you?" she says. "I am not a part of your family. I am not even human. You must feel that we are too different."

I look out the window. The landscape is eerily still. I imagine the three of us as a family, Father, Mother, and Son. Instead of being soothed, my heart aches at this image. I can't identify the source of this ache anywhere in my memories. I mutter, "He must really love you, to confide all these fears to you."

"I find his concerns interesting. I don't receive such opportunities often. The ghosts cannot discuss their previous lives. We exist without heavy rumination. He challenges me in a way that's exciting. And I like to tell him what he wants to hear. It's fun seeing his reactions."

"You want to be human again, don't you? Isn't that what you all want?"

Madame throws her head back and laughs.

I cross my arms. Her fascination with Father and me feels more and more intrusive as we talk. I am a specimen for her to study.

"We are not so different," she says. "I've often asked these questions myself. I am the oldest entity in this region. I came into this world as an adult, and I am the only one among my peers who has stayed here. I didn't care for my past life. And when the possibility to move on from this world arrived, I refused. I wanted to continue to suffer. The complexities that loneliness and regret weave into existence are of great interest to me. I've been around for so long and yet I still find things to be surprised by. Like you and your father. How utterly fascinating, the devotion you two show each other. I once had a child myself, but I found it very easy to give him up."

"Did you hurt him?" I ask.

"In a way —yes. He arrived in this world shortly after I did. He must have been around your age. To be honest, I had no evidence that he was my child. I didn't have any memories of him. And yet I was possessed by a sense of certainty. He must have approached every ghost in this region, asking if she were his mother. I couldn't bring myself to answer him. I kept my distance. The kind of love he was asking for terrified me. I couldn't bear someone needing me that desperately. It was a love that belonged to the land of the living. Eventually, a ghost answered his call. She said that she was his mother, and she took him in, and they created a small family."

"But how could he believe her? I would never accept anyone but Father."

"You're right. Perhaps he didn't believe her. But that's the thing about kindness. Once someone decides to give it to you unconditionally, it's hard to push them away.

And they made a great family. They were very happy with each other, which meant they moved on quickly from this world. And so I was satisfied with my decision. If I hadn't stayed away, then I might have ruined their chance at peace. And I was able to pursue the eternity that I desired—alone."

I tell her how horrifying that is.

"What is? That we can't recognize the people we love?"

"That you abandoned him. You let him live a lie."

Madame frowns. I shake my head. "Why was I born here? Why do I have to be around monsters like you?"

"Isn't it obvious? You're here to dissuade the ghosts from wanting to return to the land of the living. You're here to remind them of how fearful and angry they were in their previous lives. You and your father possess a keen sense of Death. Humans like you are always thinking about him, seeking him out. A few follow that instinct and manage to find the entrance to this world while they are still alive. They find the river where all are tested and, if deemed worthy, are escorted to this side. Their arrival is a joyous occasion to me. I love to see how they will behave."

I stare at Madame in silence and take in her words. I remember how happy the ghosts were around Father, how much they smiled, how they indulged him and took him into their community. When did Father realize it was all an act? That the facade would drop once they knew he couldn't perform his role anymore?

Where has he gone?

· · ·

I run out of the attic. Ghosts are in the hall dusting the cabinets and hanging up framed paintings of Madame. They are gathering the shattered mirrors from the floor. When they notice me, they stop what they are doing and stare at me in silence. Their eyes follow my movement. They are not smiling anymore.

When I reach them downstairs, the ghosts stop fixing the grandfather clock, they stop washing the dishes, they stop butchering the rack of lamb. I head outside and the world is quiet. The sun shines in the clear sky. The grass sways on the rolling hills. Flowers lose their petals. When I near them, the ghosts stop planting seeds, they stop steering the oxen plows. It is wrong for me to know the truth. Even the children on the playground stop playing. Their faces lose a childlike innocence and they age right before me, serious and unafraid.

"Where is he?" I shout.

No one answers. The shadows remain stretched across the land.

I run and run until I reach the forest, and I remember how lost I was in there. I return to the mansion, where Madame is waiting at the front door. I demand her to show me Father.

14

We walk down the basement steps. The room is completely dark until Madame lights a lamp in the corner. "He's ready for you now," Madame says.

A dark figure lies asleep on the floor, his hands and feet shackled to the bars on the wall. I am stunned. I can't catch my breath.

"That's not him," I say. "Why does he have shackles on?"

"He put them on himself. I can't take them off without his permission."

The dark figure groans and turns to move out of the light. He faces the wall.

"Don't worry," Madame says. "I know how it looks. But he is happy living like this. It is what he wants."

I squat next to the dark figure and yank on the shackles as hard as I can. "Where are the keys?" I ask.

"He's hidden them somewhere beside him. He can get out anytime he wants."

I paw at the floor, digging my nails through the dirt. There aren't many places that he could have hidden them.

Madame walks over to me and places a hand on my shoulder. "He won't let you unlock them. This is what he wants."

"Who is he? That's not Father. It can't be."

"I'm disappointed in you," Madame says. "I didn't think you were someone who would deny what's right in front of your eyes."

"Father is strong," I say. "He is strong and unafraid. He doesn't lie crumpled up like this."

"This is who he really is. He has simply stopped hiding it from you."

"No," I say. "I know who Father is. I know he will always take care of me and the world around us."

"Take a good look at him."

"What did you do to this person? What did you say to him?"

"I simply offered a solution to his dilemma. It was entirely his choice. I did nothing to influence him."

I stagger back. "How can a person live like this? Look at him. He can't even stand up. What does he do when he's awake? It's so dark."

"I visit him twice a day, and even that can be too much for him. Look at this from another point of view. He is completely safe from the shadows now. Nothing unpredictable can happen. There is order and security. His meals are delivered to him on time. I help him bathe and relieve himself. The rest of his time is spent confronting the fears and voices that afflict him. Nothing can exacerbate those fears here."

"You're wrong," I say. "He likes being in the outside world. He used to leave the mansion every morning. I tried so hard to stop him."

"But now the shadows have taken over and they are desperate for his soul."

The dark figure moans. His eyes flutter open. He says my name, and I gasp. The light shines on his face. He looks so much like Father. He reminds me of an unspeakable memory.

"I'm so happy to see you," he says. "I thought you disappeared in the forest. I thought I heard you tell me to turn back and save you from the shadows."

I don't answer him. I can't.

The dark figure turns to Madame and says, "Thank you for bringing him."

"Of course," she says. "I promised I would keep him safe."

"You must have been so scared," he says to me. "I got lost. I kept hearing your voice. I kept hearing the ghosts. And then I couldn't move. I was so afraid. I couldn't do anything to help them. But Madame found me. She brought me here."

"How long have you been here?"

"I don't know. A very long time. I couldn't keep track of the days. How are you doing? Have you eaten? Have you had a nice time here?"

I seal my mouth shut.

The dark figure frowns. He says, "You were right all along. It's better to stay inside. I can't go out there anymore. I can't listen to the ghosts' cries for help. There's nothing I can do for them. I'm powerless."

"The shadows aren't dangerous anymore. The ghosts have returned to their normal lives. They don't need our help."

"That's because I've locked myself away. Once I'm out there, the ghosts will call to me. They will want to reunite with their memories, and their longing will give power to the shadows. As long as I'm not out there, the world will be safe."

Silence passes between us.

"It'll be like how you always wanted. You can stay in the mansion with Madame and me. We'll be safe."

The dark figure closes his eyes. His face tenses up and he starts to breathe very heavily. He cradles his head in his arms, and rocks back and forth. "Stop," he says. "It's not my fault. I just wanted them back. I didn't mean to bring us here."

I hold back my tears. I want to reach out to him, but something within me says that will only make things worse. This isn't Father. He can't be. Madame places her hand on my shoulder and says we should go. She turns off the lamp, and guides me up the steps.

I say, "Where is the real Father? Where has he gone?"

"That is your father. The sooner you accept it, the less pain you will feel."

I hear Father's laughter. Bright and free. Yes, he is out in the garden, chatting with the ghosts. He is helping them with their farmwork, and I am there too, right by his side.

15

I lock myself in the library. I refuse to speak to Madame.

She leaves me alone. She does not try to convince me to talk to her. I cannot think about Father. There is so much I don't understand. I stare at the blank pages in the books. Their stories are gone. The images are dead. I cannot arrange them in a meaningful order. What did the characters do to save one another? The thought of their fictional struggles makes me sick. They do not know real suffering. I turn off the light and am calmed. Nothing is expected of me here. I will not be forced to help anyone. I can simply sit and let emptiness fill me. I am fine with this fate for myself. I can understand why the dark figure wants this too, but I cannot accept it. I cannot think of Father as that small and weak creature.

There is a knock on the door. Food has been delivered. I carry the tray into the library and eat. It is not enough to sate me. It is impossible to stay inside this room forever. The panic that drove me to seek isolation has diminished. I am now restless.

I leave the room and hear Madame downstairs. She is talking to one of the ghosts who works on the farm. After I reach the bottom of the staircase, I walk past them

and look into the kitchen where the door to the basement waits.

Then I meet Madame's gaze.

"You're awake," she says.

I am surprised to find that I am not angry at her. I am
numb to everything.

Madame asks if I would like to accompany her on
a trip.

I nod. The outside world would be a reprieve after
yesterday. I am capable of handling its dangers. Nothing
can compare to seeing that dark figure.

Madame and I enter the farmland. I take a moment to
enjoy the nice cool air, the scent of flowers and grass. I
pretend the opaque shadows are not there. The sun warms
my face, and I breathe deeply.

"You're recovering better than I expected," she says.

We pass the wheat fields and arrive at the residence of
the ghosts. We make our way to a building that seems to
be a church. Inside, many ghosts have already gathered in
the pews. Madame directs me to an empty seat and walks
to the altar at the front.

She stands between a large marble tub of water and
a white coffin. She thanks the ghosts for attending the
ceremony. From the side door, Father's friend appears,
escorting something familiar toward the altar. The body
he guides is covered by an opaque shadow. It has no eyes,
no features at all.

Father's friend carries the faceless figure into the tub of water as Madame appears behind it. It leans back into her arms, and she lowers it under the water. It starts thrashing madly, throwing up its arms and kicking its legs out. Its muffled voice rises out of the water.

Madame holds it steady underneath, her arms stiff and unflinching. When she finally lifts it from the water, she intones, "I strip you of your name. I strip you of your attachments. It is time."

The shadow starts to recede. First from the head of the ghost, and then down the rest of his body until the entire tub of water is black with memories. The ghost gasps for air. I can see his eyes, his mouth, his disbelief at being brought back to life.

He gets out of the tub. Father's friend wraps a towel around his shoulders and moves him into the chamber behind a side door. When Father's friend returns, he lifts the tub with tremendous strength, and pours the blackened water into a coffin. He closes the lid.

The ghosts in the pews try to hide their unease. They clench their faces and shield their eyes. A few shudder with amazement.

"It is your time. It is your time," Madame says as she places her hand on the lid. Screams erupt from the coffin, and the wood sounds as if it is going to break. We sit still as the shrieking grows louder. I imagine that the black water has formed its own body and is terrified of losing its life. I imagine the pain it must feel to be separated from its host, never to unite with the ghost again. Are we no longer human if our most painful memories are lost? Are they what give our existence meaning? I should be overjoyed that the shadow has been stripped from the ghost, but my heart aches at what I am witnessing. No sounds come from the coffin anymore, but I am unsure if the memories inside have given up or have found peace.

Madame starts singing in an unfamiliar language. All the attending ghosts join her. They clasp their hands together and bow their heads. As the song continues, light radiates from the coffin as it hums and vibrates. And when the song ends, the light vanishes and the coffin is still. I know it is empty now. Father's friend lifts the coffin, and the rest of the ghosts form a line in the aisle. They file out of the side door, and I am left by myself in the church.

In the days that follow, I fill my time with farmwork as I try not to think about this power that Madame wields. I am desperate to distance myself from her and the dark figure in the basement. The reason Father was fixated on Madame and his friend is clear. More than anyone else, they belong to this world. They help it function properly. They are not plagued with human doubts. They can confront the darkest of memories and force them back into the river, preserving the peace. As long as I am busy, I do not have the energy to be overwhelmed by the shifting rules of this world.

I help cultivate the soil in the bright morning sun. The back of my neck tans into a deep brown. My hands memorize the repetitive motion of digging. I barely notice the hours passing. I am empty, empty, empty. The ghosts rarely bother me. They are focused on their own work, suppressing their longing so that the memories stay at bay. When they do interact with me, it is to give advice on how to better prepare the soil for planting or to praise me for working so hard. There is no forced conversation or laughter. Our relationship is purely professional. I try to be useful.

I realize that I was always capable of this work. When Father first asked me to join him on the farm, I should have agreed. I should not have been so resistant. I could have found a way to adjust and give Father what he wanted. Then he wouldn't have been so afraid for my well-being. He wouldn't be tormented with helplessness. I don't understand why these realizations come only when nothing can be done anymore. What use can I be to Father now? I have no clue what the solution is to the present predicament. So much of existence has been confronting the failures of my capabilities, to kneel before uncertainty. I am capable, I say to myself. I am strong. I am not afraid to suffer. I will find a way.

During my lunch breaks, I head to the playground where the children are usually playing a game. I ask if I can join, and they say yes. We chase one another, and I am focused on tagging the next person, on evading the person who is "it." At the end of the game, they like to tell me I am very fast. "You should play soccer with us too," they say. "You can join my team." Nothing is hard about this. Compared to Father and Madame, the children are simple and pure in their motives. All I have to do is play.

Twice a day, during lunch and dinner time, Madame visits the dark figure.

I have started to stand near the stairs and watch her enter the basement with a tray of food. I wait there until she returns to the kitchen. When she sees me, she nods and smiles. She never asks me to join her on these visits, and afterward she leaves me alone and continues on with her affairs.

Her work requires her to meet with several different ghosts throughout the day. I assume her primary responsibility is to direct ceremonies for the ghosts afflicted with shadows. But not every ghost can be saved. Madame seems to sense something inside the ghosts beneath the shadows. What is unclear to me is how she determines which ones are ready. From what I saw at the ceremony, success depends on the ghost's relinquishment of their longing to live inside the past.

One evening, Madame isn't present to deliver the dark figure's meal. I suspect a case is keeping her occupied. She has assigned one of the ghosts in the mansion to make the delivery, but I do not feel comfortable with the intrusion of this new presence. I decide I've kept my distance for long enough. That I am ready to face the dark figure.

I run into problems almost immediately. Without Madame to lead me, the darkness of the basement prevents me from finding solid footing on the steps. The light from the kitchen can barely penetrate it. My foot slips and I furiously grip the railing to regain my balance. The tray of food wobbles on my palm, but thankfully nothing spills over.

Then it takes me a considerable amount of time to find the lamp. My sense of direction is distorted, and I am nervous about stepping on the dark figure. He makes no noise at all. He doesn't snore. His body doesn't rustle against the dirt floor.

"Madame?" the dark figure says. His voice is quieter and raspier than last time.

"No, it's me," I say.

He shouts my name, and his happiness unsettles me.

"The lamp is to your right," he says.

I find it, and when the light shines on the dark figure, I see how thin he has grown. How pale and weary his face has become. I place the meal next to him and say, "Have you been eating all your meals? If you don't like the food, I'm sure Madame can bring you something else."

"The food is fine. It's delicious."

"You should eat everything on the plate," I say. "There's not a lot of it already. A bite or two isn't enough. You need your strength."

"I'm eating everything, I promise. I still have a big appetite. This is just from the lack of movement. I've lost some muscle mass."

"You have to get up and move around then. There's plenty of room."

"You're right, you're right," he says. "I've just been tired. I get a little faint when I move around."

"Are you really Father?" I say, panicking, my breath caught in my throat.

"Why do you look like that? Of course I am. I'll start to move around soon. Then I'll be good as new. It's not hard to regain my strength. You're worrying too much."

I scoop up a spoonful of soup and feed it to him. He swallows and smiles. "It's delicious. I'll have some more. I can feed myself. You can relax. It's my food, I'm an adult, I can do it on my own."

As he eats the soup, I break the loaf of bread into tiny pieces. I cut up the apple and then worry that it might be too hard for him to chew. I remind myself to ask the cook to put grapes or orange slices on the tray instead of apples.

The dark figure asks me how my stay at Madame's mansion has been. I say it has been great. I tell him how nice and thoughtful Madame has been. I tell him I've been working on the farm and have adjusted well. I am not afraid of the ghosts like I once was.

I watch the dark figure's face carefully, trying to see if he shares the same memories as Father.

"Really?" he shouts. "That's wonderful. That's so, so wonderful. Tell me more. Tell me everything."

I go on. I talk about the ceremony. I talk about the ghost trapped inside the shadow of its memories. How the water turned black as the ghost came back to life.

The dark figure listens. And as my visit continues, he grows more tired. He lies on the ground. His face tenses and his body stiffens. Still, he makes an effort to continue our conversation. He smiles at me.

"They're quite amazing, aren't they? Madame and that ghost. I couldn't believe it when I first met them. The shadows are afraid of them. They can touch the shadows without being consumed. It must have to do with their lives in the living world, the kind of people they were. They must have been sent here to protect this land."

"Father was sent here to protect this land," I say.

He smiles and his eyes express deep sadness. "I can't protect anyone. I've only been pretending to be strong, but the shadows must have seen through my act and taken away my powers. I've always been so scared."

"You can't be Father. Father would never behave like this."

He turns grave. "You have to accept what I've become, Son. You can't change how sick I am now. It is wrong to resist fate."

Before I can respond, he crawls to a corner of the room and digs in the dirt. He pulls out a key and unlocks the shackles. I am filled with terrifying hope. But he does not point to the stairs. He asks me to help him up, and we move into the alcove where the latrine is. He needs to squat over it, but his legs are too weak for him to stay in that position for too long. I hold him as he relieves himself. The smell of feces fills the air. I close my eyes and hold my breath. "I'm sorry," he says, his voice heavy with shame. Time passes slowly. He leans onto my shoulder. My arm is wrapped tightly around his waist. "Are your legs sore?" I ask. "Can I do anything else?" I grab the toilet paper and help him wipe. "I'm sorry," he says again, and I try to do a good job so he can feel clean and comfortable.

We move back into the main room. He lies on the floor, and I pull the shackles out of his reach.

"You have to put them on me," he says.

"You don't need them. You're already stuck in this room."

"They keep me safe from myself," he says. "I don't want to ask you again."

The dim light from the lamp deepens the lines on his face. I can sense his anger rising. I do not understand. I put the shackles on him and he says, "Thank you." I bury the keys near him and turn off the lamp and bring the tray back to the kitchen. I am surprised by how easily I can navigate the space now. Behind me, his voice rises up in sobs, aching and full of remorse, as though he is talking to someone from his past. No, that cannot be Father trapped down there, avoiding the world. That cannot be the person I have known.

16

From then on, I visit the dark figure every evening, and try to better understand him. I feed him. I rub his legs and back and arms to circulate blood and prevent sores. I help him relieve himself. We chat about my daily routine, although there isn't much to say. Nothing new happens. I start to get used to our predicament. I am still unsatisfied with the situation, and I always have hope that he will change his mind and leave the basement. But I do not get angry and frustrated anymore. I find satisfaction in seeing him smile and enjoy his meal. This is not a bad way to exist, I tell myself. There is not much difference between how he lives and how anyone else lives. The days are repetitive. There is little to do. The outside world is simply another room in the mansion to be confined to.

I ask Madame if there is any chance he will join us in the living room. If he will walk into the outside world again.

Madame says no.

We are in the attic. It is late at night, but the ghosts are still working. They are about to burn the field to help the next batch of crops grow. They're in the midst of clearing away the dry matter around the edges of the field so the fire will not spread beyond that area. The weather has not been too dry or rainy. The wind is not too strong. The conditions are perfect tonight. When they finally light up the field with torches, the fire is small and spreads slowly. I am amazed that things are going so well and the fire is not burning out of control. The ghosts know what they are doing. They can bring order to even an unpredictable phenomenon. Madame and I watch the fire for a long time.

For the past week, she has been quiet. Whenever we eat together or encounter each other around the mansion, she seems to hold back her thoughts. As in my conversations with the dark figure, Madame and I stick to banal topics such as the weather or our work around the farm. I suspect she wants something from me. I can't think of another reason why she would allow me to stay in her mansion and be so kind to me. She is patiently waiting for the moment of action to come.

"What have you decided?" she asks.

"Decided about what?" I ask. "What can I do?"

"There's plenty you can do," she says.

"What are you saying? I'm a child. I can't help this world."

"Something has to change. Things have been too calm. I sense it. You sense it too. Acceptance is not the right path, even if it seems like the easiest one. You are destined for a greater role in this world. I see the ghosts meet the same fate again and again. I have no hope for them to change. But with you, transformation is possible. You must open up this world to us in a new way. Otherwise . . ." she says.

"Otherwise? Will you throw us out of your mansion?"

"I have many options. I'm still considering all of them closely. Just prepare yourself. Either you act and bring a new order to this world, or the shadows will."

My chest rises.

The fire outside is dying down. The flames shrink until there is only smoke, which blends into the darkness of the night. The ghosts check the field for last bits of ember to smother before they gather their equipment and head home. I am afraid of what I must do.

Madame has too many cases one day and assigns me a household to interview. She senses that these ghosts are under threat of being possessed. I say I am not prepared for such a role, and she gives me a look that conveys I do not have a choice in the matter.

She says all I have to do is spend the evening with the family, talk to them, and then document my observations on how strong their longing is for the past. She trusts that I will make the correct assessment.

"Don't tell me you're still afraid of us?" she asks. "They won't do anything to you."

"I know," I say.

"From what I've heard, the ghosts on the farm have taken quite a liking to you. They tell me you work very hard."

"That's nice of them. We don't interact a lot."

"Now come on, have some confidence. You're a part of the community now. They practically treat you as one of their own."

I frown. I don't want to hear any more of this. I can exist here only if there is a clear division between me and the ghosts. I don't have any room inside of me to feel sympathy or fondness for them.

Madame is quiet. She squints and furrows her brow. Then she relaxes her face and says, "I look forward to hearing about your visit."

After I knock on the door, I stand patiently, but no one comes to answer. I wait. I can't hear any indication that there is someone inside. I walk slowly around the house, tapping on the windows, shouting for them to let me in and that I've been sent by Madame.

I wait for so long that the sun starts to set and the ghosts return home from the fields. As they pass, they give me strange looks. I want to explain that I am not an intruder. I am here on an assignment. I do not know how much longer I can wait, but I hate the idea of returning to the mansion without accomplishing what has been asked of me.

Eventually, a ghost approaches the house and greets me. He says his name is Joe. He is an older gentleman. Balding, gray mustache, a cane to keep him upright. He smiles warmly at me and asks if I've been waiting long. I say I arrived only a few minutes ago. I explain that Madame has assigned me to conduct the examination.

Once we are inside, he shouts, "Marie, where are you? The examiner is here."

No one answers him. We sit at the table, and he pours me a cup of tea. "That's strange," he says. "She should be home. She's taken time off work to take care of our child now that the shadows are near. I'm sure she's here somewhere. She wouldn't leave Augustus all alone."

We drink tea and nibble on cookies. I glance around the room, feeling nervous and restless. I wish I didn't have to intrude on their lives like this. "Wait here," Joe says, and he walks into one of the rooms. The walls are thin, and I can hear most of what is said.

Marie hisses at him, "Why did you let him in? He was just about to leave."

"You need to come out. This is no way to treat an examiner. What if he tells Madame about your behavior?"

"I've done nothing wrong. Augustus is getting better. That's what I wanted to tell you. It's a false alarm."

"That is enough. We can't keep him waiting anymore."

"Dad?" The child coughs.

"Look at what you did. You woke him!" Marie says. "Oh, honey. Go back to sleep. You need to rest."

There is a long silence before Joe returns to the living room and tells me that Marie will be out shortly. I am close to telling him that I don't need to carry out the interview. That perhaps we can reschedule it for another day. But I don't know what I would tell Madame, and a conversation with her would be much worse than one with Marie.

I numb myself in preparation for our discussion. Joe and I continue to drink tea and eat cookies. From the adjoining room, the child cries and cries. Marie comforts him. Joe and I don't acknowledge the noises. We talk about how the newest batch of crops is doing on the farm and the challenges the other ghosts face at work. We soon run out of things to talk about. I know I should start asking questions about his child, but I have the sense that it would be too painful for him and I would receive very little useful information.

The windows dim and the room darkens as day turns to night. Joe strikes a match, and holds the flame near the wick of a candle. He carries it to our table, and I start to feel tired as I watch the light flicker.

Finally, the door creaks open and Marie comes out of the room. "You're still here?"

I say that I need to give Madame my report. I cannot leave until I have observed the child.

"There's been a misunderstanding," she says. "Augustus is fine. I haven't seen the shadows recently. You should report that to Madame."

"Marie," Joe says, frowning. He looks tired too. He wants this to be over as soon as possible.

"I just got Augustus to rest, Joe. We can't disturb him right now."

"I won't be long," I ask. "I don't even have to talk to him. I just need to see him."

"That's not possible tonight," she says.

Joe sighs. "He has been here long enough. Marie, let him do his assignment."

"What's wrong with you? Don't you care about Augustus? The shadows are not anywhere near us!"

Joe shakes his head. He stands up and walks toward the room. Marie lunges at him and pulls on his arm. "Get away from there! He's sleeping. Let him sleep!"

Outside the house, odd noises emerge. At first, I assume it's only the wind whipping the leaves and branches, but then in the corner of my vision, I notice a thick shape in the window. The shadow is so much more opaque than the night. Moonlight cannot penetrate it.

Joe pushes past Marie and manages to open the door. He faces me and says I can go in. I glance at Marie, and her gaze holds me back. Her expression is so strained, I can't bear it. I get up. I can't spend another minute in this place. I need to work quickly.

The shadows outside let out a deep groan. The light from the candle behind me leaks into the bedroom. Through a window, moonlight streams down onto where the child sleeps engulfed in a blanket. He is even smaller than I thought. Half my size. He shakes violently as his eyes move under their lids. He mutters words I can't understand. It is clear that there is no point to an interview.

"Don't take him," Marie pleads as she rushes into the bedroom. But I know she is not speaking to me. Joe comes and holds her as she screams at the shadows. "We barely had any time with him. It isn't fair. He needs to stay here for a little longer. Why are they taking him?"

I sit next to the child and place my hand on his head. It is burning. He is in immense pain. Marie can try and try, but nothing will wake him up. This child's existence will end in this room. I close my eyes and Father's voice comes to me. Try to understand them. The child writhes underneath my touch. I open my eyes, and tell Marie and Joe that I can help them. I can show them memories of their past life.

Marie and I enter the forest. "We have to be quick," she says. "We can't leave them home alone for long. They need me."

The night surrounds us. I am unsure of the source of my courage. I simply feel as though I have no other choice. I can't be helpless any longer. I steel myself against fear and take deep, even breaths.

When I begin to worry if I have led us in the wrong direction, the sounds of rapid river currents fill my ears. I hold Marie's hand, and we push forward as shadows growl from behind the trees. Soon we reach the entrance to a cave that I know contains the river where all memories gather. It calls to us, welcoming our arrival.

Inside, the golden light emitted by the river guides us through the darkness. The cave is full of voices whispering indecipherable things into my ears. Are they calling for our help or warning us to turn around? The journey is strangely easy, and I wonder if the real trial will begin at our destination.

On the shore, Marie steps onto the boat, and I launch it into the water before heaving myself aboard. I grab the oar and slowly row us deep into the center of the river. Marie holds out her hand, and I wrap my palms around it. The golden light of the river begins to tremble like some great machine. I can sense that I have done the right thing. I am on the right path to fulfill my role. To save Father.

Marie wavers. "Wait, not yet, I'm not ready."

"This is the only way to keep the shadows from taking your family."

She hesitates and then asks, "What's going to happen? Shouldn't Augustus be here too?"

"No, it's you. You're the one plagued by longing," I say.

And then the water, with its golden light, rises all around the boat and wraps us inside of a sphere. Before Marie can reply, we leave this world. We enter the realm of memory.

I am in a clinic from Marie's past. The foreign land of the living.

Marie is weeping. She is weeping tears of joy as she stares at the image on an ultrasound machine. I feel everything she feels. I know everything that she knows. The doctor moves the device over her stomach and tells her that the baby is healthy. The thing right there, in the center of the screen, is her heart beating steadily. The doctor tells Marie the results of the checkup. Everything is going well. Her pregnancy is right on track. Marie can't stop crying from relief. This is her third attempt to have a child and she has been preparing for the worst possible scenario. She can't be blindsided by loss again. She will never recover from another unfathomable shock to her heart. The air is dense with joy. The weight of this one moment is suffocating. It stains an entire lifetime and colors every other experience. She believes that nothing else will ever compare to the euphoria of hearing the doctor's news. No, she thinks forward to one other experience. Her baby's birth, the success of the pregnancy. The clear, definitive end to her fears.

It never comes. The baby's birth never comes. She never reaches the bliss of that sublime moment. The doctor's visit bleeds into another memory, and the air darkens. The smell of blood permeates the room. Contractions, but it is too early. Pain, unimaginable pain, but it is too early. The baby's body has not fully formed. Marie faints. Her husband finds her. He drives her to the hospital. The doctor decides she needs to perform surgery to remove the baby in order to save the mother. Darkness, and the inescapable smell of blood again, this time cut with chemicals, the burning of tissues and sinew. She wakes up in anguish. The baby suffered from a mysterious illness. Marie never hears the name because she is screaming as the doctor talks. She wails. Not only in this memory, but in the afterlife.

I am back in the boat. Marie convulses in my arms. Her screams darken the golden sphere of memory. The shadows thicken and close in, suffocating us. Is this how we will spend all of eternity, frozen inside of her screams? I am responsible for this. I brought her here. I invoked the memories. I have to be the one to guide her back to herself. I have to face the terror. Please, let me find this strength. Please, let me become someone I am not.

I squeeze Marie's hand and close my eyes. Suddenly, the screams disappear and everything goes quiet. When I open my eyes again, we are somewhere else. Marie is far away from me. The sun is setting. But there is still light.

"Bell," Marie says, "where are you going?"

"Just a few more minutes. I want to keep playing."

"It's getting dark. It's time to go home. Your father is expecting us."

"Tell him to drive here, and then he can take us home."

"No, that's not how this works. We made a deal. We go home at seven. You can't go back on your word."

"But I'm having fun. It's not fair. Why can't I stay out here all night?"

"The playground will be here tomorrow. You can come again."

"What if it isn't here tomorrow? What if it disappears?"

"Then I'll take you to another park."

"Will it have a playground this nice?"

"Of course, and if it doesn't, I'll drive you to another one, and if you don't like that one, then I'll drive us to another one. It'll be a road trip."

"You're lying. You can't drive me anywhere. You're dead."

"I can still drive us."

"No, you can't. You won't be here tomorrow. And the park won't be either."

"I'll always be here. I'll always wait for you."

"Don't make promises like that," Bell says.

"You've grown so much," Marie says. "I can't believe how big you are."

"Will you really come back?"

"I'll try."

"I won't be the same. I'll probably be bigger next time, and I'll be able to stay out as late as I want. You won't be able to tell me what to do."

Marie laughs. She wipes her tears.

"You're going to leave now. You're the one leaving. I'm not going anywhere."

"Yes, I have to go. I can't stay here."

And then Bell disappears.

Marie stands under the setting sun. The dim light gives me the sensation that this moment is different from her other memories. I am unsure if it is even a memory, if we are in a realm outside of the living and the dead.

The next time I see Marie, she is lying in my arms. She is weeping, but it is different. She has brought herself out of her darkest memory. She spoke to the person she needed most. The opaque shadow dissolves around us. And the golden light shimmers in the river beneath the boat. Marie says, "Thank you, thank you for showing her to me."

But it wasn't me. *I* didn't do anything. I was more afraid than she was. I'd accepted our demise, and I'd given myself over to the madness of the shadows. I am still trapped inside of the scream. My senses are numbed. I imagine eternal consciousness inside of a body unable to feel. I am cold. I am so cold.

17

As we walk away from the river, Marie cannot contain her enthusiasm. She retells the story, cherishing every detail about Bell. Her brown hair, her cherubic face, her white clothes. She says that she recognizes the park they were in. It was a park near Marie's childhood home. She wonders if it still exists in the world of the living. She is excited to return to Augustus, because she knows he will be better. She knows their family will be spared. The shadows cannot touch the hope alive and beating inside of her.

I am tense the entire time she talks. I keep my gaze forward so that I do not have to look at her. I do not know how she can so easily forget about the darkness and the scream. I try to smile for her sake, to nod and play along. But there is danger all around us. We do not know what will result from my actions. If I have let something snarling and hungry out of the river.

"Can we return here again?" Marie asks.

"Again?"

"Yes, how else will I see her?"

"Marie, I don't think it was the right decision to come here."

"But it worked. You saw for yourself. I was reunited with the child I lost."

The shadows around us snarl and snap. Marie holds on to me tighter, and we walk faster toward the opening of the cave. I can sense that something within her is feeding the shadows. Longing. Her hunger has only strengthened. I realize how intricate Father's work is. Our darkest thoughts can appear in many forms. They can be delusions that inhibit us from confronting reality. Marie is thinking too much about the world of the living, the sort of life she could have had. She is deathly attached.

We exit the cave and walk slowly through the forest in order to catch our breath. Things are quieter now, and the trees sway calmly. But as I try to find the way back, I realize that I don't know where to go. The confidence I felt when I first entered the forest is gone. Every direction looks the same. I can't tell which way will lead us home. Marie points to a section of the forest ahead that looks familiar to her, but when we reach it, she shakes her head and says she is wrong, she doesn't know the way either. I am close to panicking, but I don't for Marie's sake. She is as frightened as I am, constantly glancing over her shoulder. She holds herself together by placing faith in me. I start to shout, hoping someone from the mansion might hear us. Madame must be searching for us. I should have arrived home long ago. The only thing that brings me comfort is the absence of shadows. The trees retain their vivid shapes, and darkness does not stifle our senses. Marie joins me in shouting for help, and finally, to our surprise and delight, someone calls back. We run toward the speaker as he steps forward and pushes the branches away from his face.

I gasp. I am filled with the most remarkable joy. The trees seem to shimmer in his presence. It is Father. He approaches us. His face is full and beaming. His limbs are long and muscular. He looks young, like he did when things were normal and we were safe together in our mansion. He opens his arms, and I run into his embrace. He picks me up and swings me around. "I've found you," he says.

"You're out of the mansion. You're in the outside world," I say.

"Of course. I heard you calling for me. I couldn't let you get lost."

"I knew the figure in the basement couldn't be you. I knew the real you was living somewhere else."

"Yes, you were wise to distrust them. I've been in the forest the whole time. I haven't been able to leave."

"This whole time? How long have you been here?"

"Ever since that day when we first entered the forest, when we got separated."

"But I found you. You led me out."

"That wasn't me. That was something else."

My eyes widen. I try to go through my memories, but the connective tissues between them crumple. They're like discarded pages. Where am I? What have I been seeing?

Father grabs hold of my hand. He places it against his chest. "It's me," he says. "Can't you feel it? My flesh. The warmth from my heart. I've finally found you."

Father smiles down at me, and I bend under the enchantment. Yes, this is what I want. Father's love. His total attention. No more confusion, no more distractions. Only his devotion. I am happy. The feeling is as genuine as it can be. Father has returned to me.

I turn to face Marie. I am excited to tell her that everything will be OK. The shadows can no longer harm us. Father regained his powers. He is strong and brave again. He can resume his role in this world.

I leap toward her, desperate for someone to share my enthusiasm and tell me I am right, but when I come near her she backs away. A gruesome sound falls out of her mouth. She is shaking and hunched over. Her legs appear as though they will give out. I try to talk to her and calm her down, but she can't stop staring at Father. Her eyes bulge, her face is pale. Horrified, she pushes me out of her way and flees. She disappears into the darkness of the forest, her footsteps echoing until they are too far away to hear.

I am frightened too. Something must be following us. Something must be near, lurking right behind Father. I sense his warmth beside me. He kneels down, and places his hand on my shoulder.

"We should go after her," I say. "She might be in danger. She shouldn't be alone."

"Go after her?" Father says. "But she's a ghost. Why would you want to help her?"

"Yes, but she's different. She has a daughter. She just wants to see her again."

"Is that what she told you? How can you believe her?"

"I saw it. I saw everything that was precious to her."

"You're being *tricked*."

"What?"

"The ghosts are master storytellers. They can easily spin the most elaborate tales to gain your sympathy, and once your guard is down, that is when they strike. You know all of this. You know not to blindly believe them."

"But she was scared. She wasn't trying to hurt anyone. She ran away because she saw something in the darkness."

"She ran away because she knew I'd caught on to her tricks and wasn't going to allow her to deceive you anymore."

"Father . . . ," I say, trembling, "there's something I've been told. *You* told me this. That there is a greater threat in this world. There are these shadows, they are our memories, and they are hunting us. They want to consume this world and plunge it into darkness and despair. And you, you're supposed to—"

"Shadows?" Father says, and he frowns. He looks mournful. "You must be very confused. It is such a shame that the ghosts have taken advantage of you like this, and I wasn't there to help."

"But I've seen the shadows. I've seen how they take over the ghosts and their world."

"You're so deep within their lies you don't even realize it," Father says and embraces me again, stroking my back. The warmth of his body calms me on this bitterly cold night. "They're very close to reaching their goal. Once they've broken us with their stories, we won't have the will to stop them, and they'll be free to use the river to cross into the land of the living. That has been and will always be their goal. Our strength is all that maintains the border."

"The land of the living . . ." I say.

"Come now. I'll show you when the time is right. But first you must free yourself from their illusions. You must see them for what they really are."

Father guides me through the trees and tells me the mansion will appear different with my newfound knowledge. Once we are at the edge of the forest, he says that he cannot cross over. He will lose his strength if he is near the mansion. The ghosts have used its magical resources to cast an enchantment over the land that will ensnare him if he comes too close. I have to make the journey on my own. Only I can seek out the truth before they grow too suspicious.

I ask Father if we really have to separate again, and he says that we can't be together until the ghosts have been forced back into their rightful place.

18

During my return to the mansion, I immediately notice that the surrounding landscape has returned to normal. Dense shadows no longer cover the area like sun spots on a photo. Or rather the landscape has always been untainted. The shadows existed only in my mind, and Father has freed me from my delusions. I can't believe how relieved I am to walk across the grass unimpeded.

I must first pay a visit to Marie's home. I am worried she has not found her way home. I want to clear up any misunderstandings and explain to her that there is nothing to fear. But then my chest tightens and my pulse races. I remember Father's warnings. I don't want to be further deceived by the ghosts' tragic tales of loss. And yet I can't turn around. My body moves on its own. I want to find out the truth for myself. Because within my heart, I still possess a fondness for Madame and Marie and Joe and Father's ghost. They have all been kind and patient with me. Can emotions be manipulated so easily? If they can be, couldn't everyone—ghosts and humans—be tricked into happiness? Why is sorrow painfully difficult to let go of?

No one opens the door. I knock and call out their names, but Marie and Joe's home remains silent. The curtains on all the windows are drawn. Perhaps Marie and Joe are out on the farm with a recovered Augustus. I wait for a few more minutes, watching the sun cast pale, harmless shadows across the ground. I hear the shuffle of footsteps coming from inside their home, and a muffled voice that has Marie's distinctive lilt. I know I must turn around and walk away. The door will remain closed no matter how long I stay.

As I pass through the farmland, the ghosts are performing their regular duties. They till the land. They guide the oxen. They feed the livestock. When I approach them, I find a change in their behavior. I wave and greet them, and the ghosts stop what they are doing and stand rigidly, staring at me as though possessed. They discard their shovels. They hold the oxen in place. They drop their bags of feed. And they back slowly away from me with a frantic look in their eyes. I do nothing in response. I am deeply disturbed by their unease. I watch as they flee. I have never seen them abandon their duties like this, not when the sun is shining, and the sky is clear, and the land promises sustenance.

I look at my hands. I examine my body. I do not understand. I do not see what they see. I wonder if they know that I have learned the truth about their deception. Yes, they are finally leaving me alone. This should thrill me. There should not be this tightness in my chest. My heart should not ache. My legs should not shake. Yet, I find my eyes searching, restless and ravenous, for someone to come toward me, smiling and affectionate.

I visit the playground. I order the children to gather around me. A few try to turn and run away, but when I raise my voice they freeze and follow my orders. They are different now too. They have stopped laughing and smiling. They cry and plead for me to let them go. I am surprised by my voice. It seems to come from a place outside of me, but I feel my mouth move and my throat vibrate with viciousness. "Come play with me," I say. "Don't you remember how much you wanted to play?"

"It's getting late. We have to go home."

"There's still time for one more game," I say. "I promise it'll be fun."

"Our parents will be worried."

"You'll be in more trouble if you don't stay."

The children form two lines and link hands. I stand in the middle of them. I say we're playing Red Rover, but in my version, only I get to run into them, and whichever line breaks first will lose.

"We don't want to play," they say. "We want to go home."

"Then hold on tight," I say. "Whoever loses will never go home. You'll have to play with me forever."

They cry harder and whimper, "Stop it, stop it, someone's going to get hurt," but they are obedient children, and so they keep holding hands. They play along.

I hurl myself into a line, and they scream, and I'm smiling, I'm giddy, no matter how much they plead, I can't stop, something else is in control, I'm trapped in a distant region of my mind, watching from behind a shut window, unable to control the actions of my body. As I run, I see the fear in their faces. I see how weak they are. I don't understand why I am doing this.

I wish I could believe this is not who I am, this intense glee I feel when I inflict harm and wield power, but I am forced to consider that this *is* who I am. This raging, resentful side of me is just as vital and vibrant as that fearful little boy hiding behind walls, acting out to feel less helpless. There must be a way for these different selves to coexist within me. I can't hide from them. I can't run away.

The children sense a crack in my resolve and break out of my spell. They say enough, let go of one another's hands, and run off over the hill back to their homes where they will be safe.

19

When I reach the mansion, Madame and Father's friend are not there. They are always out working tirelessly to peel the shadows off the ghosts and save them. The baptism process takes too long, and they cannot reverse the transformation as fast as the shadows consume their prey. Memories of the living are everywhere. They destroy anything in their path as they haunt us. It will be only a matter of days until the whole world is an abyss. The ghosts shelter at home in an attempt to save themselves, but they must sense that the shadows' reach is unending.

At least this is what I've been told. A tale that still has a hold over my heart, even after Father lifted the enchantment and the hallucinations of shadows dissipated. How can Madame and the ghosts go to such lengths to deceive me? How can their emotions feel so sincere? They work with such devotion to save this world. I cannot understand what they gain by living inside a lie.

Lately, Madame's demeanor has changed. She is grim and barely speaks to anyone. Before she leaves to perform baptisms, she always looks as though she wants to ask me something, but stops herself with a shake of her head. The disappointment on her face causes me to shudder. She acts more like Father's friend, who has always been cold and unaffectionate to me, keeping me at bay as though I am only an obstacle to accomplishing his work.

As I walk around the mansion now, I find that I miss them both. I do not want to believe that we must be enemies. I don't want to assume the worst in their intentions. The pounding of metallic chains from the basement interrupts my thoughts, and I wonder if I am still deep within the ghosts' scheme. If I lost my way long ago.

I walk down to the basement. I dig the keys out of the corner of the room and unlock his shackles. The dark figure does not move. I pull him into my arms and carry him up the stairs. Mere weeks ago, this would have been impossible. But he has grown so thin and light that I only have to take a few breaks. His shoulder blades jab my chest. His legs rattle against each other. I am horribly afraid that if I drop him, his body will break apart before my eyes. He moans and shifts in my arms.

I set him down on the sofa, his head on the armrest, his limbs stretched out. I call out to him until he wakes up. He winces and shields his eyes with his hand.

"You're free now," I say. "The shadows are gone. They were never even there. You don't have to hide."

He stares at me in horror and recoils. "You're here," he says. "You've finally come for me."

"I've always been here. I've visited you many times."

He shakes his head. "But I've kept my promise. I gave up my powers. I stopped helping the ghosts."

"Who are you talking to?" I ask. My eyes ache and my vision blurs.

"Leave me alone. You shouldn't be able to get in here."

His fear darkens the air. The crazed way he looks at me unravels me entirely. He claws the sofa, and pushes himself onto his feet, but as soon as he takes a few steps, his legs give out, and his body collapses with a terrible smack. I hear bones crack.

"Stop it," I shout. "Why are you doing this?"

I grab his shoulder. He jerks away and slaps my hands off him. "Go away, you can't take me back. You can't have my soul."

"You're going to kill yourself," I say. "You're going to get yourself killed."

The dark figure doesn't look at me. He continues to crawl toward the basement. He reaches the stairs, and drags himself down the first steps. He slips and careens forward. I hear a series of thumps and the horrible sound of his body slamming into the stone floor. I let out a screech. I am desperate to know what he is afraid of. I feel myself losing control again. I run down the steps and impulsively pull him into my arms. He doesn't fight back. He is losing consciousness. I carry him into the center of the room and put the shackles back on him. His body is covered with deep bruises.

"Spare them, please," he says. "You can take me, but you have to spare them."

I gaze deeply into his eyes, and say, "I am safe. Everyone is safe. There is nothing to fear anymore."

Shortly after I return upstairs, the front door bursts open. Madame enters the mansion with Joe, Marie, and Father's friend. When she spots me, Marie has the same expression from the forest. She points at me and trembles, clutching Joe's arm. "It's him," Marie says. Everyone stands rigidly, their guard up. Father's friend approaches me slowly, like he would with a wild animal. Madame extends her arm in my direction and says, "Don't move."

"It's *me*," I say.

Before I can react, Father's friend lunges and restrains me with his arms around my chest. He lifts me up as I scream and struggle, punching and kicking at the air. Joe comes forward to help Father's friend, but Madame stops him. She says he can't touch me.

Father's friend drags me up the stairs and into a bathroom. Madame, Marie, and Joe follow us without offering any sign that they'll help me or hint that they're making a mistake. This is the true nature of the ghosts, I tell myself. Father is right. Now that they know their lies have been exposed, they do not pretend to be kind anymore. They will do anything to weaken me and Father so that we can never interfere again with their plans to access the world of the living. I despair at having fallen for their act. I despise my heart for ever hoping that they would treat me as one of their own.

"Let me go," I shout. "I know the truth. I know what you really are."

In the bathroom, Madame fills the tub with water. She mutters an incantation that causes it to boil and glow. Father's friend dangles me over the water. I beg them to stop. Madame orders him to proceed, and he plunges me into the water. The heat sears my skin. The air leaves my lungs. I fight as hard as I can, pushing myself up, gasping for air, but Father's friend is so strong, he tightens his grip on my shoulder and he presses me under. Marie is wailing, and Madame shouts, "I strip you of your name. I strip you of your attachments. It is time. *Repent.*"

The water grows hotter. It chokes my throat, it burns my eyes. I have to destroy them. I cannot let the ghosts survive. They will never let me live in peace as long as we both reside in this world. I claw at his hands. I bite down on his wrist and taste blood. Father's friend hisses and loosens his grip. I crawl madly out of the tub and stare at the color of the water. I am petrified.

I don't want anyone to see me like this. I run past Joe and Marie, who rush out of my way. Behind me, Madame shouts, "It's not working. He's going to get away." I'm already at the bottom of the stairs. They can't catch up to me. I sprint out of the front door. Water falls from my body, darkening the ground below me. I don't look back.

20

In the forest, I find a patch of foliage to hide inside. I pull the branches and leaves over me and hug my knees to my chest. I let the forest hold me still. I feel safe in the darkness. No one comes for me. I let my panic drain into the dark. The vines and branches thicken to protect me. Nothing can get in. No one can find me. I empty myself. I empty my heart. I am safe. I have nothing to be afraid of. The day passes into night and the night presses me to the earth. There is no moon, no stars, no animals. I have all the time in the world. I have no worries, no responsibilities. I am free. I am a child.

"Now do you understand?" a voice says. It is Father. I am sure of this. I turn my head from side to side, but I cannot see him. His voice seems to rise up from the soil, cold against my ears.

"Yes," I say.

"They mean to do you harm. The world around you is not safe. Everyone you meet is treacherous, spinning tales, and you cannot trust them. You can never let them into your heart, or they'll use you until you're broken. You have to stay by my side, forever, so that I can protect you."

"Yes, Father."

"Then you know what you must do. You must free yourself. Take away the ghosts' source of strength. They'll be lost. They won't be able to interfere with us again."

I nod. I push the branches, and they give way easily. I stand up, and the path back to the mansion presents itself to me. I have no doubts. My whole being has firmed up with resolve. I walk without hesitation. The forest is deeply quiet again. I can hear only the sounds that my body makes in the dark.

I stand in the burned field. The smell of char still lingers. Ash covers the soil. It stains my knees and hands when I kneel on the ground. The wind scatters the gray flakes. The ghosts said the field would recover and plants would grow back. But that is hard to believe when the land looks the way it does now.

I make my way to the supplies shed. I pick up the equipment I need.

21

The edges of the mansion stink with gasoline. I've poured out as many cans as I could find.

I stand on the lawn and look up at the attic window, the only source of light visible from the outside. The mansion is so quiet. The land is so quiet. All living things have fled.

I throw a lit match onto the front steps. I back away. Flames burst up. They grow and grow, burning the mansion, blocking the only exits.

I feel the heat on my face. The walls start to crack. Wood planks snap and smash onto the ground. Behind me, something wails and writhes. Something is traveling up the hill toward the mansion.

The fire will break through the door and consume the ghosts. This is what we all want. An ending. Painless. Definitive. I've finally made the right choice.

Then—I am seized by panic. I see the dark figure, awake, screaming and screaming, as light fills him and reduces him to nothing. I hear those horrible screams so vividly, and I realize that he will have to watch the fire come for him, he will have to feel the immense pain of the fire on his skin, and I can't stand this thought. I can't understand why he means so much to me.

I charge through the front door. The fire grips me. The heat scorches my skin. The beautiful order of the mansion is in flames. Parts of the ceiling cave in. The stairs collapse. In the kitchen, the cans explode. The books in the library crumble to ash. I run past the burning furniture and reach the steps to the basement.

"It's too late," a voice says behind me. "You won't make it."

I feel myself losing strength. The burns on my skin are unbearable. There is the possibility that I will lose consciousness before I even reach the dark figure. The steps seem to extend endlessly. The fire has followed me into the kitchen and is catching up.

I land on solid ground. The dark figure is sitting in the corner, staring blankly into the air.

I say his name. I say it again.

My voice reaches him, and he blinks. Our eyes meet. He is precious to me. No matter the other confusion I feel, I am certain that I have to be by his side. We are whimpering and afraid, but we are together. I hold on to him tightly, and I say I am sorry. I say I don't know why I've done this to him.

His voice is soft and kind. He says, "It's time. Things will change. This is the moment I've been waiting for." He shushes me and rubs my back. Even as the fire engulfs us, he does not stop comforting me. Even as the pain consumes me, I can still hear him, I can still feel him beside me. The end is here. And we will be gone from this world.

22

When my eyes open, I am lying in a boat on the river of golden light. The dark figure sits beside me, holding onto the oar. I sit up, and my body is still my own. There are no burns on either of our skin. I turn my head and see the people on the shore. Father's friend, Madame, Marie, and Joe, and countless other ghosts stand and watch us.

"You're awake," the dark figure says. His voice aches. He rows us further down the river. "They saved us. They helped us when it seemed like all was over. We have not been alone like I assumed."

"You're not afraid of me?" I ask.

He shakes his head. "I can see you now. I finally realized it, when I was about to lose you."

The boat drifts farther from the shore. The ghosts fade into the darkness of the cave. I wrap my palms around the dark figure's hand. "What are we going to do now? There's no longer a place for us in this world."

Right then I sense that the night has consumed the entire world. There is only this river, the boat, and us. Outside there is nothing but madness, longing, and loss.

The dark figure says, "I know what to do. Do you trust me? Can you do one last thing for me?"

"I don't know," I say. "I don't know what is right or wrong anymore. I'm lost."

"Yes, you do," the dark figure says. "It is time. You will go to the world of the living. You will live among your own people and find your way."

"That's not possible," I say.

"We are the ones who connect the dead to their memories of the living, and we are also the ones who escort them across this river when they first arrive. It is within our power to return when the time calls for it. And you are not like me, you deserve the chance to have a life of your own. I'll stay behind. It is my responsibility to restore this world. You've given me the strength to do so."

"I can stay and help. I don't want to leave."

The dark figure embraces me. I can't bring myself to call him by his real name. Things are too different now, so much has changed. I am afraid of the emotions that saying his name will bring out of me, of the life that we've lost. He lifts me up and lowers me into the golden light beside the boat.

I grip him tightly, my arms wrapped around his neck. The light is so cold. I can't let myself fall into it. "Will I see you, or Madame, or any of the ghosts again?"

He smiles. "Of course you'll see us again."

"I don't believe you. I can't leave."

"You have to. You have to move on. I can't protect you here anymore."

I don't respond. I am frozen with fear.

"We'll see each other again," he promises, and smiles, and then plunges me into the golden light.

I stay deep inside of the river until I can't breathe and am desperate. I claw and kick toward the surface, terrified of Death, and hungry for life.

I break through the water.

I grab the nearest object I can find and hold myself up. When I kick out my legs, they hit a hard barrier, and pain shoots up my body. I open my eyes, and look down. The water is shallow enough for me to sit upright and stay afloat. I squeeze my fingers. I squint and I am filled with unease. I have not resurfaced from the river. I am not in the cave anymore.

I am sitting in a white porcelain bathtub in a familiar room. Water trails off my torso as I step onto the floor. I run my fingers across the smooth wood paneling, taking in every detail of the room. This can't be right, I think. How can the air smell so similar? I stand in front of the sink mirror and touch my cheeks, my mouth. I keep expecting to see some creature other than myself in the reflection.

The water in the tub remains clear. I towel myself dry and find clothes in one of the cabinets. Outside of the bathroom, a hallway lined with doors leads to stairs. The size of the hall, the paintings on the wall, the location of the staircase, everything is the same. Sunlight hangs in the air, and I observe the shadows lying beside the furniture. How calm and quiet. How frighteningly ordinary.

At the end of the hall, a bedroom door opens and a little boy runs out screaming. He is half my size. He is so young, perhaps the age of a toddler. His black hair shines. Sweat drips down his panicked face. He passes by me as though I'm not there. Can he see me? I raise my hands. I look down at my body. Didn't I use the towel to dry myself? Didn't I put on real clothes? The boy races down the stairs. It isn't long before he returns, pulling another person up with him. As they approach, I see that the person is an older man. Father. The resemblance is unmistakable.

I follow them to a room. They kneel beside the bed where a woman is lying down. She appears to be the same age as Father, but her body is thin and malnourished. An IV tube trails from her arm to the bag of fluids hanging from the metal stand. Her skin is pale and the bones in her face jut out. She keeps her eyes closed no matter how hard the little boy tugs on her arm. She is asleep. No, it is much worse. She is dying. She reminds me of the dark figure in the basement. Her body is so weak that she cannot move. She cannot leave the room and run free into the outside world again. That is when I see her shadow stretch toward me. I lean over to touch it, and the surface is cold and rigid. My hand shakes.

The boy and Father are trapped in their panic. Father holds a phone to his face and shouts for an ambulance. The boy climbs onto the bed and curls up against her side. He lifts his head and says, "Mom. Mom." He is so young. I try to remember what I looked like at his age. Father argues with the operator on the phone. I want to look away.

Why am I here? Why do I have to witness them like this? But I know I cannot leave. I cannot abandon them. I have to see them rescue her. I have to see them find happiness again.

"Do it, then. Offer them salvation. Offer them an end to their suffering." It is the same voice from the forest. The one who goes by many names. Death.

I stare at the window above the woman's bed. Thick, heavy fog pollutes the view. Dark shapes thrash in the distance.

"She has already crossed the river. But there is still time. They can still run after her and bring her back to the land of the living. Show yourself to them. Point the way."

I breathe deeply. I find myself swayed by this voice. I imagine the look of bliss on their faces. I imagine how they can finally be a family again. How they will never have to be separated.

The little boy weeps by the woman's side. Father holds her hand and sweeps the hair out of her face. Fog blackens the window.

"Of course, they will be tested on the other side. If they look back as they lead her out of the cave, their souls will belong to me. You must prepare them well. You must guide them through their doubts and longing."

The ambulance siren rings out, its light penetrating the fog and filling the window. The little boy and Father get up and stare out at the world.

"You're running out of time. If they leave this room, if they leave the mansion without you, they'll never have the chance to find her soul again."

"They'll look back," I whisper. They'll get lost on the way. They won't be able to tell what's right and wrong. They'll look back to check if she's there, if they have been tricked throughout the journey. I know the myth.

"You don't know that. You can change the past. You can change what they become."

The boy and Father turn their heads and look in my direction. They don't recognize who I am. They see only the version of me that Death is showing.

"Go on, save them."

I open my mouth. I cannot help myself. I offer them the choice. I know the path it will lead them down. I know that they will fail and their time together will bring only more pain. I give them the chance, and they take it. They are exuberant. They cannot see the future that I am in. I have done my duty. I let them chase after what will ruin them, their bodies alive with astonishment as they charge forward into the fog.

Acknowledgments

Thank you to Zoë Koenig and Lizzie Davis for picking this manuscript out of the slush pile and championing it. I was only able to finish revising the novella because of their support and insights into the story. Coffee House Press was the only place I submitted the manuscript to, and so without them, this book truly would have never existed. I am still in disbelief that I am a part of this family.

Thank you to the entire team at Coffee House Press, especially to the people I had the privilege to interact with. Thank you to Carla Valadez, Abbie Phelps, Marit Swanson, and Daley Farr for playing huge roles in bringing out this book.

Thank you to my teachers at Syracuse University. Thank you to Mary Karr for teaching me that writing can serve a larger purpose and enrich life with meaning. Thank you to Dana Spiotta, Sarah Harwell, Christopher Kennedy, Jonathan Dee, Arthur Flowers, Brooks Haxton, Bruce Smith, and Michael Burkard. I wrote the first draft of the novella during the MFA program, and I can't imagine writing it without my experiences there.

Thank you to Kundiman, the organization that has been with me from the very start of my writing journey. I'll never forget how Sarah Gambito, Joseph O.

Legaspi, and Cathy Linh Che invited me to my first writing retreat full of Asian American artists. Due to Kundiman, I never questioned whether creative writing was a possible path for me. I was exposed to so many inspiring Asian American writers that I naturally believed I was capable of writing a book one day.

Thank you to Ariel Chu, who has read more of my work than anyone else in my life. I am so grateful that I am able to call someone as generous and gentle-hearted as Ariel my friend. I believe that I will always have an audience for my work thanks to how much care Ariel puts into reading my writing. Thank you to the 312 Allen crew, Zeynep Özakat, Joshua Burton, and Anthony Veasna So. My writing life has changed due to your friendship.

Thank you to Ralph Sassone, my first writing teacher. Thank you for taking my work so seriously and giving me valuable feedback and guidance. I was able to see a future for myself in the writing world thanks to you.

Finally, thank you to my parents, Ngat Tran and Nguyen Vo.

Coffee House Press began as a small letterpress operation in 1972 and has grown into an internationally renowned nonprofit publisher of literary fiction, essay, poetry, and other work that doesn't fit neatly into genre categories.

Coffee House is both a publisher and an arts organization. Through our *Books in Action* program and publications, we've become interdisciplinary collaborators and incubators for new work and audience experiences. Our vision for the future is one where a publisher is a catalyst and connector.

LITERATURE
is not the same thing as
PUBLISHING

Funder Acknowledgments

Coffee House Press is an internationally renowned independent book publisher and arts nonprofit based in Minneapolis, MN; through its literary publications and *Books in Action* program, Coffee House acts as a catalyst and connector—between authors and readers, ideas and resources, creativity and community, inspiration and action.

Coffee House Press books are made possible through the generous support of grants and donations from corporations, state and federal grant programs, family foundations, and the many individuals who believe in the transformational power of literature. This activity is made possible by the voters of Minnesota through a Minnesota State Arts Board Operating Support grant, thanks to the legislative appropriation from the Arts and Cultural Heritage Fund. Coffee House also receives major operating support from the Amazon Literary Partnership, Jerome Foundation, Literary Arts Emergency Fund, McKnight Foundation, and the National Endowment for the Arts (NEA). To find out more about how NEA grants impact individuals and communities, visit www.arts.gov.

Coffee House Press receives additional support from Bookmobile; the Buckley Charitable Fund; Dorsey & Whitney LLP; the Gaea Foundation; the Matching Grant Program Fund of the Minneapolis Foundation; Mr. Pancks' Fund in memory of Graham Kimpton; the Schwab Charitable Fund; and the U.S. Bank Foundation.

The Publisher's Circle of Coffee House Press

Nghiem Tran was born in Vietnam and raised in Kansas. He is a Kundiman fellow, and he has received degrees from Vassar College and Syracuse University. *We're Safe When We're Alone* is his first book.

We're Safe When We're Alone was designed by
Bookmobile Design & Digital Publisher Services.
Text is set in Adobe Caslon Pro.